"Night sailing really turns me on."

Stephen said nothing more for a long time, although there was a lot that Anne wanted to say—and do. But no, they didn't know each other well enough . . . yet. She contented herself with snuggling closer in his embrace.

"I love your arms around me," she murmured at last.

Stephen lowered his head next to hers, as if only sensing that she'd spoken.

She tried again, but the wind took her words away. Settling back against his broad chest, knowing Stephen couldn't hear her, she finally indulged her fantasy. "I wonder what it would be like . . . to make love out here."

"Fantastic," he whispered directly into her ear. "I'd bet on it. . . ."

Nothing about **Alicia Fox**'s life has been ordinary. Her pursuits have included skydiving, raising two pet monkeys, operating a "beer bar," working on a defense project in Washington and surviving alone for a year in the mountains. All Alicia's adventures have finally led her to a contented life as wife, mother and talented new writer. And we predict that readers will be sharing her love of excitement for some time to come.

Legal Tender

ALICIA FOX

Harlequin Books

TORONTO • NEW YORK • LONDON
AMSTERDAM • PARIS • SYDNEY • HAMBURG
STOCKHOLM • ATHENS • TOKYO • MILAN

Published April 1987

ISBN 0-373-25251-X

Printed in Canada

1

AFTER HAVING DROPPED everything on a moment's notice to drive across town in noonhour traffic, Anne Michaels had finally run out of patience. "Okay, Trudy, what's behind this 'urgent' luncheon of yours?" Her friend had been sitting there in smug contemplation, and Anne was beginning to resent feeling like a goldfish under scrutiny.

Trudy took a deep breath. "I've been judging your mood. Will you hear me out before you draw any conclusions?"

Anne sat back. "As long as you don't go on any more harangues about where I could possibly expect to be five years from now."

A slow smile of guilt surfaced. "Well, actually, all those 'harangues' did have a purpose. I was sort of using you, and your situation, to help me make up my own mind about something."

"Oh, terrific." Anne didn't bother to hide the iciness that crept into her voice more frequently these days. "I hope I was of some service."

"Oh, you were," Trudy assured her, not even acknowledging the sarcasm. Instead she continued to ponder her own thought. "Anne, I think I have a plan that'll be the perfect answer to both our problems." Trudy could be so cocky.

"Ah, let's have it." Anne decided to humor her. "But let me warn you, if it's supposed to justify the torturous encounter-group tactics you've used on me in the past five days, I'm expecting to hear the equation for life, at the very least."

Trudy dismissed the comment with a wave of her hand as she leaned across the table to speak a little more intimately. "Well, for starters, I've decided to take a six-month leave of absence to go back to Oregon and have my back surgery."

Anne's expression became one of genuine relief. For once the conversation wasn't going to dwell on Anne's increasingly precarious career. "Well, it's about time! Congratulations, Trudy. When?"

"Soon," she said. "But that's not what this little meeting is about." Once again, Trudy grew philosophical.

"Anne, after a week of picking your brain about why legal administration means so much to you, I realized something. Here I am, sitting on one of the most exciting law-firm-management jobs in Los Angeles. I got it on a real fluke, and if I turned loose of it at this point, I'd never be able to get another one like it. Instead, I'd be right back in the exact same position you're in—stuck between a rock and a hard place with all my upward mobility routes closing year by year, right before my very eyes."

Anne actually fought back the tears on that one. Had the woman lost all sensitivity? After a week of hearing Trudy use phrases like "swimming upstream" to describe Anne's future, she just didn't need any realistic comparisons, as well. "So, let's get to the bottom line," she urged, glancing at her watch.

Trudy took a deep breath of resignation. "Well, I also realized it's that job of mine, and that job alone, that's been keeping me here in Los Angeles."

"So? What's wrong with that? A career is pretty important. You've got a rather unique situation at K&W." Anne laughed at her own understatement. "I mean, getting to design every system and procedure for a newly created forty-man law firm isn't exactly what I'd call an everyday opportunity."

Trudy leaned back and shook her head. "That's true. But you know something, Anne? I don't want it. I just don't like city life. I want to go back to Oregon and stay there."

The woman hadn't lost her sensitivity—she'd lost her mind. "But you'd be a fool—" Anne's voice cracked, and she impatiently cleared her throat. "Trudy, a year ago you were at half your current salary, managing a little twelve-man firm. Then, just because they happened to get swallowed into a bigger one, somehow your typical Irish luck put you in a position any one of us would kill for. And you're thinking of walking out on it?" This was like dying of thirst while someone else was taking a long, leisurely shower.

A coy little smile touched Trudy's lips, and she looked Anne straight in the eye. "That's what this luncheon is about. Do you want my job, Anne? Because cut it any way you want, I don't."

"Oh, sure." Anne grimaced. "Now she's playing God."

"I'm quite serious."

Anne looked at her a long moment, and she finally shook her head. "Trudy, don't take this wrong, but as you say, you fell into the position on a fluke. Obviously if you ever quit, they'd do what all the major firms have started doing. They'd bypass all us obsolete ladder climbers and pull another M.B.A. type right out of private industry, and it would be one more marriage in the clouds, beyond all our reach."

Trudy's lips curled in almost patronizing amusement. "And I'm telling you that at this point, the partners who make decisions at K&W still think like small-firm people." She leaned across the table. "Maybe if little Anne Michaels would be willing to take a crap shoot for once in her life, she just might step from being the office manager of a nine-man firm to being the administrator of a forty-man firm. In one swell foop!"

Just hearing those words made Anne's heart jump into her throat. Working her way up to such a position through normal routes could take years, if she ever made it.

"I shouldn't even ask this, but just out of idle curiosity, you did say crap shoot."

Trudy raised an eyebrow. "Well, I'm not giving notice at this point, you see. I'm simply taking a leave of absence. So one risk is the scant chance that I'll change my mind about coming back, and frankly, I can't even imagine that, so give it a 99.6 percent margin of safety. Otherwise, it would just be up to your performance and your ability to endear yourself to a bunch of extremely provincial personalities over a six-month period—while you're a 'temporary fill-in' for me, of course. Trudy winked."

"A temporary *fill-in*?" Anne slowly set down her coffee cup. "And what, may I ask, do I do with my job during the six months that I'm babysitting yours?"

"Well, obviously you'd have to quit."

Anne laughed. "Quit Mendelson, Hanes & Roberts?" The woman really was mad. "Trudy, how often does *any* management job surface in the legal community? Even in a small firm, for heaven's sakes. I mean, I know a lot of equally qualified people who envy my job evey bit as much as I envy yours."

As Anne listed her protests, she heard the pace of her own words steadily quicken, and a slight note of panic was creeping in. After all, the thought was clearly preposterous. Anyone could see that. Couldn't Trudy see that?

Finally Anne interrupted herself. "You're suggesting I leave a good, solid stepping stone of a job that I've held for five and a half years? And for—"

"For a fluke," Trudy provided meaningfully. Again that familiar little smile. It was the same one Anne had noticed every time she'd watched her friend go after something impossible. And then get it. "So?" Trudy taunted. "Want to hear more?"

Finally Anne threw up her hands. "No, I don't want to hear more. You're crazy! What else can I say?"

But Trudy just grinned. "Try 'uncle.'"

SIX WEEKS LATER Anne Michaels stepped out of the elevator and, as always, marveled at the imposing impression two names could make if they were set in raised, bronze lettering against a dark, paneled wall. Kimble & Watson, Attorneys-at-Law. The words hung there, practically commanding reverence as they cast their shadows on the rich wood behind them.

When Tracy, the receptionist, looked up, she immediately waved a finger in the air. "Anne, wait a minute." Punching the hold button on her phone, she reached for a pink message slip.

Anne's eyes dropped to the name, and her eyebrows drew together in puzzled surprise. "Merrifield? I thought he wasn't due back in town until next week." As far as Anne had understood, K&W's superstar had been locked into a grueling deposition schedule in Philadelphia. Since he was putting on a big push to jam all the depositions together without any breaks, it seemed rather odd that he'd be in Los Angeles right in the middle of all that.

The receptionist raised her eyebrows. "All I know is that he stepped out of the elevator around twelve-fifteen looking as if he'd come straight in from the airport. Then, without even so much as 'hello,' he asked me if his secretary was out to lunch."

Tracy lapsed into a warning whisper. "When I told him Eileen was home sick today, he told me to buzz you, and without even waiting to hear that you weren't in, he disappeared through the door. Ten minutes ago he called me and asked where the hell you were, as he put it."

Anne looked at her watch and then hurried down the walnut-paneled hallway. It was twelve fifty-five, and those minutes could tick by very slowly for someone who was frustrated and waiting.

Entering her cozy inside office, she saw another message on her phone, hastily scrawled in heavy black ink. "Please call S. Merrif—" The rest of the signature was a straight line.

All right, I'm coming, she thought, dialing his extension.

"Merrifield," he sighed, sounding harassed.

"This is Anne Michaels." She kept her words as clipped as his.

"Give me twenty minutes and then come by."

"Certain—" He clicked off halfway through her short reply, but she replaced the phone in its cradle, unoffended. That was the first unspoken law-firm motto she'd learned—"Let's be abrupt! It may be rude, but it's fast!"

Anne's eyes dropped hopefully to the three messages that had been left on her desk while she was out. Nothing important. She grimaced, setting them down with a bang of disappointment. That was something she and Trudy hadn't counted on. During the whole four weeks she'd been at K&W, the partners had given her almost nothing to do. Other than an occasional errand, the firm seemed to be operating on its own without missing a heartbeat.

All of a sudden the thought hit her that maybe she was being seen as little more than a baby-sitter, to be kept on the shelf until Trudy returned. That certainly wasn't part of the plan, but as long as K&W was under the impression that Trudy was coming back, the partners might not give Anne much responsibility. And without that, she couldn't very well use the six months of Trudy's proclaimed leave of absence to prove herself by "being brilliant," as Trudy had put it.

Anne's eyes fell once again to Merrifield's message. Hopefully he, at least, would need more than five minutes' help with something. She was used to working under pressure, and anything to break her boredom would be a welcome change.

If only he isn't one of those hectic types who blames everything on the closest person around, she thought. The one thing she didn't need at this point was any negative publicity.

Anne continued on to the ladies' room. As she finished washing her hands, she glanced at her small gold watch. She was more than curious to meet Stephen Merrifield, if not a little nervous. Not only was he Kimble & Watson's litigation heavyweight, but the case he'd been working on in Philadelphia was a huge, messy antitrust matter that had made a big splash in all the newspapers since its inception.

Considering the sterling reputations of the three firms that corepresented the plaintiff, there had been some raised eyebrows when the lawyers had suddenly brought in a single outside litigator from another firm. But apparently Merrifield had something the other three firms didn't think they could do without, because he'd sure been retained at great expense, according to the figures she'd seen.

"A natural litigator" was one of the phrases Anne had heard to describe Stephen Merrifield. There had been other words of praise, but the one that had seemed incongruous was "sensitive." From what Anne had seen in her career in law firms, the typical litigator was a tiger looking for a scratching tree that bled.

She smiled to herself. Considering "natural litigator" and "sensitive" in the same breath, she wondered if he would have black velvet gloves. Over his claws perhaps? He'd also been referred to by one of the secretaries as "roughly elegant."

That was another incongruity. Everything she'd heard about Merrifield definitely painted the picture of a maverick. Yet he'd somehow earned the reputation for being one of the more conservative of the younger partners.

Anne mentally prepared herself to switch into high gear on a moment's notice. *Who knows,* she thought sardonically, *maybe this will be my only chance to "be brilliant."*

As she ran her comb through a soft wave of light brown hair, Anne's glance fell on the laugh lines that surrounded the turquoise eyes she'd inherited from her mother. At least the creases gave her the look of a full-fledged adult.

When they'd first appeared two years ago, she'd taken the hint of dressing more conservatively. Especially after attending her first management association luncheon. One look around that room had made it clear that if she ever wanted to get anywhere as a law-office administrator, instead of the small-time office manager of a nine-man firm, it was time to start dressing like one.

From that point on it had been classic, conservative suits accessorized with a few pieces of unimposing gold jewelry. Dress for success, she'd decided. And it worked. The difference she immediately saw in the way people treated her confirmed that the shopping spree and the shoulder-length cut should have taken place long before they did.

When Anne approached Merrifield's office, the door was closed. There was conversation inside, but it sounded like a phone call. She knocked softly.

"Come in!" The words barely interrupted his sentences.

Anne opened the door to the large, windowed office, immediately shocked to find a huge, rugged-looking man standing behind the desk. He looked as though he'd be more at home climbing a mountain than talking on the phone with a forefinger comically poked in his other ear.

But as soon as Merrifield's eyes met hers, Anne noticed a flicker of surprise before he masked the expression. He motioned to his client chair with his elbow and a nod, and then watched her. Just from the casual, assuming way he did that, she knew Stephen Merrifield felt quite at home with anything he felt like doing.

His glance neither dismissed nor openly appraised her, but Anne couldn't fail to notice the undisguised, curious interest as he watched her cross over the richly patterned Persian rug to the chair in front of his desk.

At first she felt self-conscious under the dark-eyed scrutiny, and a flush threatened to surface out of nowhere. But as soon as she was seated, Merrifield closed his eyes and squinted, as though he'd missed hearing something.

Feeling that it was momentarily safe to look at him, Anne got a mental flash of his massive body contrasted against pillows and down comforters on a king-size bed. She willed her thoughts to the present and began rearranging the papers in her notebook.

Merrifield was clearly having trouble hearing the person on the other end of the phone, and he turned to look out the window as though Anne were a distraction. It was an altogether pleasant response to evoke, and the movement also gave her the chance to study him unobserved.

Anne had expected him to look so much different! An untouchable, Aryan, Mr. Perfect type. Tall, thin and lanky, with angular lines defining features and torso alike. Instead this man reminded her of a big, powerful animal, casually restrained.

Rich, dark brown hair matched the eyes that had penetrated hers. Neatly groomed yet rugged, he had his hair cut in a style that was masculine and uncontrived, the kind Anne preferred to see on men.

Still safe from being caught, she let her glance drop to his shoulders. Their breadth seemed almost out of place in a business shirt. Anne had the amusing thought that instead of him wearing the shirt, the shirt seemed to wear him. "Roughly elegant." That secretary who had described him should be a writer, Anne decided.

She continued to watch his movements as he talked. There was nothing delicate about them, yet she could somehow picture the man removing a splinter from a baby's finger without causing a murmur. Suddenly Anne had the strangest sensation that her heart was beginning to beat differently.

As Merrifield began wrapping up his conversation, his eyes caught hers. For just a split second, Anne saw an unmistakable quality of playfulness dance through them before she forced her glance back to her notebook.

When he finally hung up the phone, he remained standing and leaned across the desk to extend his hand. "Stephen Merrifield," he said. His grasp was firm yet gentle, as though he was being careful not to hurt her.

"Anne Michaels," she replied. She couldn't understand why she kept feeling like blushing, and she hoped he couldn't see the struggle.

Merrifield straightened again behind his desk, seeming to silently remind himself of the business at hand.

"Well!" he began. "I'm only going to be here long enough to untangle a personal mess that's come up, and then it's back to Philadelphia. I understand my secretary's out, so I'm going to need some help from you." In one sentence he'd become the lawyer again.

Merrifield waited only long enough for Anne to open her notebook before he started talking. "Unless there's someone available in-house, I need a temp in case I have something today and tomorrow. I'll be out of the office for several hours this afternoon, but I'd like her here when I return."

He took a deep breath, running his fingers over a strong but well-shaped jawline, and Anne sensed a touch of weariness in the gesture. "Tomorrow I can't predict at all," he continued, "but somehow in that time I'd like to meet with Stern, Watson and Cooper. They're probably running on tight schedules of their own, but at least get an idea of flexibilities—maybe we can cross paths in some reasonable way."

Merrifield absently watched her jot little notes as he continued even more rapidly. "I also need word processing available for about a two-hour project. It'll come to them in dribbles late this evening or tomorrow, but I'll need it finished by tomorrow night, so try to line it up so they can fit me in without much notice."

He wasn't even waiting for her to write any longer, but as he talked Anne noticed the way he rubbed his eyes with his thumb and forefinger. Without knowing why, her heart went out to him.

"Also, can you give me a paralegal to summarize two depositions that I'm going to dig out of another case—I'd like to take them back with me, and they're probably three hundred pages, as I recall." He paused to look at his watch.

"Let's see. I want the paralegal to start on it right away, and if she doesn't think she can finish it tonight, get two of them on it—three, if necessary. I want it typed tomorrow."

The man seemed totally oblivious to the unlikelihood of pulling all those people together with no warning.

Anne took the moment necessary to finish her rapid jotting, relieved that he was through. "Okay," she answered simply.

A short pause was followed by an abrupt laugh of sheer delight that resounded in rich, mellow tones through the office. "That's what I like," he said, "someone who doesn't panic."

Anne caught the note of irony in the way he stressed "doesn't," and she sensed that it related to whatever had brought him back. But at least the statement showed that he was aware he might not get everything quite as readily as he'd asked for it.

Hoping not to have to disappoint him, Anne gave him a reassuring smile as she rose to leave.

But at the doorway she had an afterthought, and she turned to him. "Have you had any lunch? Tracy said you'd come straight from the airport, and—"

"I haven't, and I'm starving and thanks for asking," he interrupted. "Get one of the boys to go downstairs and get me a sandwich, would you? I don't care what kind—you pick it, okay?" He reached for the phone, but his tone wasn't dismissive; in fact, he acted as though he was quite used to having her around.

As soon as Anne rounded the corner she exhaled, suddenly aware that she'd practically been holding her breath. If *that* was the charisma she'd heard about, she could certainly understand why it got attention. The man was awesome just standing there, not to mention what he could do to a person with those eyes. Anne shuddered at the thought of having him on the other side of a deposition table. Yet the playfulness she'd glimpsed made her suspect that a shudder wasn't the only response he could arouse, given the right circumstances.

THE SECOND ANNE GOT to her desk she swung into action. It was good to have a challenge, even if it was only a short-lived exercise in coordinating people. Besides, anything could become interesting if it meant talking to Stephen Merrifield again.

Figuring everyone was back from noon breaks, Anne called the secretaries of the three partners Merrifield wanted to see.

The only one who gave her any problem was Jean, Mr. Cooper's secretary. She haughtily corrected Anne's request for Cooper's schedule by asking that Anne provide a list of times Mr. Merrifield would be available instead. Having encountered this game before, Anne used the easiest ploy, sympathy.

Finally Jean acquiesced as if granting an unheard-of exception, and Anne couldn't help but wonder if Mr. Cooper really wanted to be protected from his own partners to quite that degree.

After another hour of running around making arrangements, Anne went back to Merrifield's office. His door was open, with two young associates inside.

When she peeked in, Merrifield held up a finger, motioning an interruption to what sounded like a litigation war story.

"Just a report," she said, letting her expression show it was nothing urgent.

"Come in and have a seat. I'll be just a second." He returned his attention to the associate, who happily resumed.

As Anne watched the trio, she noted that both the associates looked as if they were in the presence of divinity, hanging on Merrifield's every word and hoping to impress him with a few of their own.

When they had left Merrifield motioned for her to have a closer seat, and that unsettling, playful quality came into his eyes once again. It was so subtle that she was certain he wasn't doing it on purpose. She tried to ignore it.

"Okay, I think you're all set up," she began lightly. Tiny chains clinked softly against a hollow gold bracelet as she flipped open her book. She didn't trust herself to meet the dark, compelling eyes she felt examining her every move.

Anne listed one compliance after another to his impossible timing requests, and after the feat of getting word processing to fit him into Mr. Tomlin's rush, she glanced up and caught a smile playing over his lips. What thick, black eyelashes for such toasty brown eyes, she thought.

Quickly returning her gaze to her notes, she continued, hoping to stifle her infuriating urge to blush. "Here's a list of times when Stern and Watson are free. Mr. Cooper's going to be less . . . flexible, but I reserved two sure times that he'll be here tomorrow morning."

Having covered every point, Anne met his eyes as she handed him the note and closed her book.

"Wonderful." The single word expressed surprise as well as relief. "There's been a change, though. Instead of this afternoon, I'll be out of the office tomorrow morning, so see if Jean can give you some times for today instead."

Merrifield grinned slightly at the expression of dread that must have crossed over Anne's face. "I know," he said, reading her mind. "But she types well."

With that, he lifted an accountant's briefcase jammed with heavy files and plunked it onto his desk as if it weighed nothing. Pulling out a huge stack, he let it drop on his desk with a bang. "So here the fun starts." He sighed, running his fingers through his hair.

"Well, let me know if you need anything else," Anne offered, rising to leave. She thought she felt his eyes on her as she neared the door.

"Incidentally," he added in a slightly more intimate voice, "are you just incredibly effective, or hasn't anyone told you that nothing falls together that easily in a law firm?"

Anne turned slightly in the doorway. "I use thumbscrews. Works every time." But the warmth in his eyes was too compelling, and she shrugged admission. "If you really want to know the truth, I welcomed something to do beyond waiting for a light bulb to burn out."

"Mmm." He frowned. "Now that would be an unforgivable waste of a clearly marvelous resource." There was just the hint of a teasing smile before he returned his attention to the files on his desk.

As Anne left his office and walked back to hers, she couldn't help but wonder what "personal mess" had called him back from Philadelphia with only a few more days of deposition remaining.

It had to have been urgent for him to rush home like that, yet it seemed strange that something that urgent could get casually postponed till tomorrow. She wondered if he was married.

Oops. Put that question out of your mind, she told herself, suddenly aware of where her thoughts had been going. One sure way to blow this whole Russian Roulette game with her career would be to get involved with one of the attorneys at K&W.

When Anne got back to her desk, she settled in her chair, flipping to the next chapter of the computer manual. She was just beginning to underline the chapter when the phone rang.

It was Tracy, announcing that Merrifield's temp had arrived. But it was the way she paused to clear her throat that aroused Anne's curiosity.

"Uh-oh," she mumbled as she walked toward reception. Maybe the "highly experienced" litigation secretary the agency had told her about hadn't been available, and they'd sent a beginning trainee in her place. Worse things had happened.

Anne opened the door to the massive lobby, surprised to see a sensuous-looking woman wearing a clinging jersey knit dress and a fair amount of makeup, though tastefully applied. Maybe a little more appropriate for afternoon cocktails at the marina than typing in a conservative law firm, but nevertheless, very striking.

"Hello, I'm Anne Michaels." She kept her voice officially polite as she crossed the softly lighted room.

"Janet," breathed the woman in a throaty voice that matched her appearance. "Janet Cline. I got here as fast as I could." She tossed back her long, thick, blond hair, and as she got to her feet, Anne could see that her figure left little room for improvement. The dress left little room for the imagination, either, she noted.

"You have an . . . out-of-town guest?" Janet smiled, revealing a row of perfect white teeth.

Anne ignored the look Tracy shot her from behind the tall blonde. "Well, not exactly. One of our partners was unexpectedly called back from out of town. He's trying to take care of some bits and pieces, and his secretary's out sick.

"His schedule will be kind of unpredictable," Anne continued, "so I'd like you to come in at nine tomorrow, even though he may not be here. The main thing he'll need is someone who can act as a coordinating center while he's in and out, and—"

"My best talent!" Janet interrupted. "Shall we go?"

Anne was a little put off by the way the woman seemed to take over. But at the same time she wondered why she found herself feeling so protective.

As they walked down the thickly carpeted hallway, Anne's curiosity got the best of her. "Tell me," she began thoughtfully, "when the agency told me about you, I noticed they specified that you would only take a temp assignment that was for a partner."

"Oh." Janet laughed, waving her hand. "Associates can be so boring. My forte is in public relations, and partners need more of that than just typing. Besides, I find them more . . . interesting, if you will."

Well, wait till you see this one, thought Anne glumly. She pointed out Eileen's desk before bringing Janet into Merrifield's office.

Anne thought the man's eyes would pop out of his head but, amazingly enough, he just offered an automatic, polite smile. He didn't reach for her hand, nor did he exude the interesting little touch of personal warmth he'd so readily shown Anne earlier. Instead he rose from his chair only to hand over several lists, simply asking Janet to familiarize herself with them.

But Janet's eyes were certainly fixed on Merrifield. She averted them only long enough to turn to Anne, thanking her with a definite air of proprietary dismissal.

Not failing to notice once again the way Janet's dress clung to her body in all the right places, Anne glanced across the room. "Let me know if you need anything else, Mr. Merrifield." Her voice sounded a little strained to her own ears, but she ignored it. At least it hadn't croaked.

Merrifield smiled and winked a "thanks" as he reached for the phone and absentmindedly dialed the two digits of an in-house extension. There was a look of grave patience on his face, as though he expected a long wait.

When Anne got back to her office, her phone was ringing. "Anne Michaels," she answered.

"Stephen."

"I beg your pardon?"

"Just call me Stephen," he said simply. "That's all I wanted." Then he clicked off.

2

ANNE HEARD NOTHING MORE from Stephen for the rest of the afternoon, but based on Janet's frantic calls to ask where to find things, Anne got the impression he was running the woman ragged. She told Janet to call for help if she started getting behind, but it sounded as if she had everything under control. Except, hopefully, Stephen Merrifield himself.

No one else approached Anne with any overtime requests or other mundane trivia, so she decided to bury herself in her data processing manual until five o'clock. After that she planned to go into the computer room to get some more insight into a conversion.

When Anne had first started coming in to observe, shortly after her arrival at K&W, the programmer had seemed to resent her intrusion, but when she kept showing up night after night with a genuine interest, Ralph finally began to relent by explaining the software, some of which he was designing. Now, after four weeks, he actually seemed to welcome an interested audience.

At about seven-thirty, Anne returned to her office to gather her things to go home. She was arranging a few papers and notes to herself, when suddenly she sensed someone watching her.

Glancing up, she saw Stephen Merrifield. And judging from the way he was leaning against the doorframe, he'd been standing there for several minutes. Anne felt a sheepish smile of embarrassment rising out of nowhere. *Dammit! Why do I always want to blush whenever he looks at me?*

But in the next second she became oblivious to everything beyond the twinkle in his warm, brown eyes. It seemed to penetrate right through to the back of her neck.

"You're still here, I see. You must have found some burned-out light bulbs." His voice was soft and carried no surprise, since working late in a law firm was an occupational hazard shared by all.

"Don't I wish it was because of that." Anne laughed, leaning back in her chair. She wanted to seem casual in spite of the crazed pounding in her chest. "I've been hiding out in the computer room, trying to get a feel for the little beasts." She made an exaggerated grimace of frustration. "But why are you still here, for heaven's sake? I'd have thought you'd be exhausted by now."

Stephen entered the room, his movements suggesting power even when he was tired. Without asking, he took the seat across from Anne's desk, sprawling into it like a big, lazy cat. "I've been poring through the files of an old case all afternoon, and I didn't realize how late it was. Has everyone gone home from office services?" His mellow voice echoed into the silent hallway, reminding Anne how alone they were.

"No, there are two Xerox people still in there."

"Good." Stephen glanced briefly at his watch. "Well, everything looks in control, thanks to you, so I have only one more request before I get out of your hair—can you spare one of them long enough to drive me home?"

"Mmm, I'm afraid you're out of luck on that one," Anne apologized, not wanting him out of her hair at all. "Mr. Tomlin has them waiting with bated breath to start copying a gigantic complaint. He's been finalizing it all week long, and he's spent the whole day proofing it."

Stephen rubbed his eyes. "It's a rush, of course."

"I think that would be the very least you could say about
it. It has to be filed tomorrow, and there are hordes of exhibits that have to go on it."

"Oh, yes," Stephen acknowledged, apparently remembering despite his fatigue. "That must be his favorite piece of
antitrust finally coming to its ill-fated fruition. God, I've been
so tied up with my matter that I haven't absorbed much—I
bet he's having fun with it, though," he added sarcastically.
Stephen's expression indicated the case would represent
anything but fun.

Anne laughed at the scenario forming in her mind. "The
boys are pleading with him to let them start on the exhibits,
at least. But he won't turn loose one single page until the
whole complaint is ready. He wants to keep it all together—
in his hands," she imitated.

Anne's "Tomlin voice" brought an amused smile to Stephen's rugged face. "You've got his number, I see." He shook
his head and laughed softly.

"I suppose I could call him and ask, just for the fun of it,"
she offered. "Maybe he could release one of the boys—at least
for a while."

Stephen sighed as he relaxed into a long stretch, his voice
groaning right along with it. "Nah, I'd never dream of inter-
fering in the advanced labor stages of that little brainchild.
He's probably driving himself crazy with it as it is."

One of the first things Anne had learned about K&W was
that when Mr. Tomlin was under pressure he just couldn't
stand not having a whole staff of people lined up, waiting to
step in the second he was ready. By universal understanding, everyone humored the compulsion.

Stephen groaned again as he pulled himself to his feet.
"Well, if I'm going to get home before midnight, I guess I'd
better call a taxi right now," he said, turning to leave.

"Good heavens," Anne laughed, "how far do you live?"

"Just up the canyon about twenty minutes." Then he smiled, realizing what his comment had implied. "You have to understand that Los Angeles taxicabs seem to require two hours' notice. Then they show up late." He shook his head in wry disgust.

Anne paused, her pulse quickening. *Should I or shouldn't I?* she thought. *Why not?* "Well, I'm going to the valley," she said. "I can just as easily take the canyon route over the hill and drop you off on my way, if you'd like." Her voice sounded reasonably casual, at least.

Stephen turned slowly in the doorway. "My dear, you have no idea how much I'd like. Are you sure it's no trouble?"

"None at all," Anne assured him, her voice betraying much less nervousness than she felt. "Besides, even if it were, what's twenty minutes' trouble for an office manager to save a harassed partner a three-hour wait for a Los Angeles taxi?"

"That's cute," said Stephen, scratching his head. "Well, I'd appreciate it—three exhausted hours' worth and more. Just give me long enough to throw a few files in my briefcase, and I won't keep you."

"Fine," said Anne. "I'll meet you in the reception room in five minutes."

Stopping in the ladies' room to freshen up, Anne noticed that her hand was shaking ever so slightly as she applied some lipstick. Having experienced the same tinge of turmoil all day, every time she'd been around Stephen, she was starting to feel silly. *So what's there to be nervous about?*

As they rode down in the elevator, Anne kept her eyes on the numbers as they lit in regressing order against the panel. She sensed that Stephen was studying her. Even when she wasn't looking at the tall man standing next to her, his electric presence seemed to fill the cubicle, as if every atom had been alerted to his existence.

Once inside the little white Nissan, Stephen settled comfortably into the passenger seat, stretching out his legs as he loosened his tie. There was something almost proprietary about the way he'd absentmindedly tossed her notebook into the back, and his position was such that he could watch Anne, or the traffic, as he wished.

In the close quarters Anne caught a trace of a delicious masculine scent that almost made her head swim, and she suddenly wondered what it would be like to burrow her nose into that powerful chest. *Now, Anne, there you go again.*

As though sensing her sudden need for small talk, Stephen obliged her with a neutral question. "So how's your first month been at K&W?" He seemed only too ready to think about something other than his cases for a change.

The idle chatter continued as they drove, but in spite of the growing darkness, Anne could feel Stephen's sharp gaze. He seemed to be taking in every detail, from the way she shifted the gears to the turquoise cast of her eyes when she glanced at him now and then. And every time they made eye contact, that strange feeling was there, almost as though he could see right down to her very soul. The unsettling part of it was that she liked his invasion.

As they rounded the curve before the little canyon store, Anne slowed the car. "Before I pass the market, do you need to stop and get milk or anything?"

Stephen hesitated a moment, and the car behind them honked impatiently. "Pull over a minute," he instructed.

After Anne had pulled to the side of the road and stopped, Stephen sat there a long moment. He seemed to be weighing the question in his mind. Then his eyes met hers and remained there as if he still hadn't quite reached a conclusion. "Have dinner with me," he said suddenly.

"What?" Not only was that the last thing she'd expected to hear, but a lawyer socializing with someone in-house was more than frowned upon in most law firms.

"Have dinner with me," he repeated, laughing slightly at her reaction. "I'm tired, and I don't want to go home and cook, and well . . . I won't tell if you won't."

There was a devilish twinkle of conspiracy in his eyes, and Anne couldn't suppress a grin.

Stephen kept his eyes on Anne's as though they'd just made a silent pact to rob a bank. "There's a nice little restaurant farther up the canyon," he suggested.

Anne thought for a moment. "Okay." Her voice had come out on the timid side, and she noticed the way his glance dropped fleetingly to her mouth before he brought it back to her eyes. At least neither of them had gulped.

Anne continued her way up the hill while Stephen chatted idly about Kimble & Watson, telling her a little of their history. About halfway through the merger part, she stopped hearing what he said and reflected on the effect he was having on her. Not only did she find him devastatingly attractive, but she knew that this man was different from anyone she'd ever met before.

If only my heart would stop this insane pounding, she thought, pulling into the postage-stamp parking lot to the side of the restaurant.

As they settled down at their table and Stephen ordered two glasses of wine, Anne looked around the room. The atmosphere took her back to a tiny fashionable restaurant she remembered in Paris. Each table had held a soft, delicate flower, and a violinist had played soft, delicate music. This restaurant had the same continental flavor.

The building had been a residence in its youth, and the whole room had the feeling of a canyon sun porch, with Boston ferns hanging everywhere. Some intangible feeling of intimacy seemed to bind all the patrons together, removing them from the outside world while at the same time leaving each table to its own world of privacy

Anne's eyes returned to Stephen, and she saw he'd been watching her with interest.

Sipping her wine, she returned his unwavering gaze for a long moment before she saw that this was a contest she wouldn't win. She decided to break the silence before the ever-threatening blush won out. "I've noticed you studying me," she ventured lightly, "as if I remind you of someone."

Stephen paused for a moment before answering. "No, you don't remind me of anyone," he said. But the slight reddening of his complexion gave Anne the impression that he was feeling as transparent as she had in the car. Somehow she didn't think he was accustomed to anyone seeing through him.

"Tell me about yourself," he said, changing the subject.

Anne laughed. "So that just in case anyone asks, I can say this was your only opportunity to interview Trudy's temporary replacement, right?"

Stephen's face reflected an amused appreciation of the absurdity, but he simply waited.

"Well—" she sighed "—I'm twenty-nine, I have a bachelor's in history from UCLA, and I started working for a huge law firm as a proofreader as soon as I got out of school. Then, finding I'd make more money as a secretary, I switched to the first opening that came up."

Stephen's concentrated stillness urged her to continue.

"I felt lost in the shuffle of a large firm, and I heard of a senior partner in a smaller firm who needed a secretary, so I went with them. Then, as the firm added a few associates, I sort of grew into the position of running the office."

"How did you come to K&W?"

Anne felt as though she really was being interviewed, but it wasn't an unpleasant sensation—she liked his interest.

"Well, just to keep abreast of things, a couple of years ago I started going to the ALA meetings, and I met Trudy. We became friends, and we've had lunch together regularly ever since. She told me about her planned leave and asked me if I'd like to handle her job for her while she was gone. So," she concluded, "here I am."

"What's ALA?" Anne could sense the subtle probing of a lawyer. He kept his voice soft and understanding, but at the same time he chipped away, piece by piece.

"The Association of Law Office Administrators. They meet once a month to share information about systems, procedures, equipment, salaries . . . just about everything."

Stephen raised an eyebrow. "Law Office . . . Administrators?" He stressed the word as if she'd just said "domestic engineer" for "housewife."

Anne laughed. "Law firm management *has* arrived as quite a specialized field, you know."

"Running a law firm? You mean specifically a law firm?" His unfamiliarity told Anne that he was a litigator through and through. For him nothing else existed, let alone administrative matters.

"Yep, specifically a law firm." She grinned. "After all, they do have their own set of problems that are unique." She couldn't resist chiding him, and she leaned forward, lowering her voice. "Didn't you know that attorneys are notorious for being inept at managing their own affairs?"

Stephen's laugh erupted with a note of irony. "Now that wouldn't surprise me at all." He took a sip of his wine, but just behind the playful glint in his eyes was a slightly more than usual intensity of interest. "Had you left your firm coincidentally at the same time Trudy took her leave of absence?" Once again his voice hadn't changed with the change of subject.

"Well, not exactly," she answered noncommittally. "There were a few problems, and it was just . . . time to move on." Based on the conversation so far, there was little risk of his knowing that she'd never have left a job she couldn't replace for so casual a reason, unless she had a real hope of bettering herself.

"Ah, I understand," Stephen said, misinterpreting Anne's vagueness as professional discretion. He tactfully changed the subject. "So! What do you think of our little group?"

When Anne hesitated, he added what he no doubt intended as an encouraging aside. "Don't be afraid to comment—you're leaving in five months, anyway."

I certainly hope you're wrong about that, she thought. "It seems like a really nice firm," she began. "I'm expecting to learn quite a lot while I'm there, as a matter of fact. I admit that walking right into the middle of a computer conversion looked a little scary at first, but I'm learning something about that, as well."

"So that'll be experience you can take elsewhere," he supplied.

"Well, assuming it works out that way," said Anne, fully aware that her answer had said absolutely nothing. But she was beginning to get a little uneasy about the topic of her limited stay, and she slid into a side subject.

"It's next to impossible to jump from managing a small firm directly into a large one. There are so many people out there competing for law office management positions—even small ones—that you actually have to be overqualified to get one anymore."

"So every bit of experience counts, I take it." Stephen half smiled. "But what in the world would appeal to anyone about managing a law firm?"

"Oh, everything!" said Anne. "In other businesses the concentration is on making widgets of some sort. It's time clocks and structuring everything around the widget. But in a law firm? It's all people and personalities and rushes and craziness. It's sort of like running a household full of children with diverse interests and only one car."

Stephen laughed at her analogy, as if he thought it was all too accurate.

"And of course," she continued, "there's also another little added incentive. I know at least ten administrators who earn beyond $60,000 a year—who didn't have any more background than I do when they started." Anne still liked to forget the fact that those days had just about come to an end. "An ostrich," Trudy had finally called her when she'd continued to resist the farfetched plan to slip into K&W through the side door.

"That's a rather tolerable salary for someone who started out as a secretary."

"That's right. And that's the other problem with the widget fields. They involve cost accounting and inventories and quality controls and forecasting. Without my having an awfully strong business and accounting background, my management future in any other field would be pretty limited. On the other hand, the most important part of managing a law firm is being able to satisfy the needs of—shall we say—'intense' personalities."

Sometimes attorneys liked to think of themselves as sane, but his reaction was an amused grin of acknowledgment. That was impressive.

"So," she concluded, "since coordinating people and workflow and working under pressure are the main requirements, it seemed like a good way to launch a lucrative career without a lot more education."

"Seemed? Past tense?"

The man missed nothing, and Anne laughed. "I didn't mean to say that, but yes, there's the big rub. When I started it was already competitive, but at least all the heavyweight administrators had climbed up from within the ranks. But with the trend toward conglomerating, someone let the cat out of the bag, and all those M.B.A.'s and C.P.A. types in private industry started coming in out of the rain. Without the same impressive titles after your name, it's getting harder and harder to compete."

"But not all large firms want to be run like industrial plants."

"And bless their little hearts for seeing the light. Even without 'the new breed,' as we call the M.B.A. type, there are only so many law firms large enough to have an administrator, and there's only one in each firm. That doesn't say much for the odds, I'm afraid."

Stephen raised an eyebrow. "Whew! So you're battling impressive credentials on one side of the fence and the sheer force of numbers on the other, eh?"

Anne sat back. "In a nutshell."

"But you're still trying." Stephen squinted as a smile crept over his face. "That's very interesting," he added, his thoughts seeming momentarily diverted.

Anne shrugged. "I already had too much time invested to turn back when the new breed made its invasion. Besides," she added, "I absolutely love it. If there was anything really technical about it, I'd have thrown in the towel at the first sight of an M.B.A. But based on what I see as the priorities in running a law firm right, I figure I'm as well equipped as anyone else."

Stephen took a deep breath. "Well! You sure do sound like a career-driven lady, all right. More power to you."

Anne smiled. "I guess that's true—for the moment, at least. Someday I'll want to get married and have children, but until then I suppose my career is about the most important thing in my life."

"And you'd do what—quit working at that point?"

"Well, assuming I could, of course." Anne's expression darkened slightly. "I was raised by a mother who stayed home. That was a really wonderful time in my childhood, and I'm thankful I got it. But then my father died, and without warning Mom had to go to work. It seemed that was when my childhood ended."

Stephen squinted with interest. "How old were you when your father died?"

"Eight," she said. "That's probably another reason I'm 'career driven,' as you put it. My mother wasn't very highly skilled, and she really had a hard time supporting us on what she was able to bring home. I don't ever want to be in that situation if I can possibly avoid it." In spite of herself, Anne shuddered visibly, remembering how helpless her mother had seemed, even to a little girl.

"I see," said Stephen quietly. "Well, I can appreciate that fear would add . . . just a touch to one's motivation."

Anne laughed, grateful for the light tone of his summation. It had always been a depressing memory.

"And you—tell me about you," she urged.

Stephen let out a bored sigh. "Oh, typical story," he began. "Raised in Ohio—went to college—got honors—went to law school in Cambridge—got married. Got divorced. . . . Nothing unusual."

"Cambridge—that's impressive," she said. *Divorced— that's interesting*, she thought. Anne wanted to find out more. Just for the sake of idle curiosity, she told herself.

"And your son broke a leg tackling a teacher, which brought you all the way back from Philadelphia with only a few more days of deposition left," she prompted.

"Oh, that." He took a deep, exasperated breath. "No, Cathy, my ex-wife, isn't the most stable person in the world." Stephen's tone indicated he was making the gravest of understatements. "Yesterday she staged a mental breakdown, suicide threats and all. Her family's in Boston, and she has no meaningful friends, so I had no choice but to make an appearance."

"'Make an appearance'?" Anne was incredulous at his choice of words.

"Ah," he corrected, his sensuous lips forming a wry grin. "Staging a mental breakdown is quite different than having one." Anne got the impression he'd been through a hundred of them.

"I considered not coming, maybe once and for all to let her see that these antics might just go unrewarded."

Stephen's reply smacked of deep-rooted resentment, but his proposed alternative didn't seem too unreasonable under the circumstances he was describing. "So what made you change your mind?"

Stephen's eyes shadowed as they dropped briefly to his glass. "Well, if your life hasn't gone the way you wanted it to, it's easy to blame your spouse."

Anne smiled. "And if your spouse allows it, you get to keep doing it. On the other hand, if the old adage is true that we make our own luck, you can't feel responsible for someone else's downfalls unless you directly cause them."

"That's true. But then sometimes it's not so clear-cut." Stephen remained quiet a moment, seeming to ponder a picture in his mind. Then he shook his head. "That's all I would need," he said, more to himself than to Anne. "A guy picks a suicide threat as the time to draw the line on his ex-wife's fire alarms, and she goes out and does it." He took a slow sip of his wine.

"But you decided not to go see her today, after confirming that it was 'antics'?"

"No, nothing that reasonable." He sighed. "I called her doctor this afternoon before leaving for the hospital, and he told me to hold off.

"Apparently he put her into one of those group therapy sessions yesterday, and someone said something that struck home with her. She was uncharacteristically quiet and pensive after that, and then this morning he found her sitting in her room, looking out the window with sad tears dripping down her cheeks." Stephen must have read the expression of concern on Anne's face. "That sounds like something to worry about, but in her case it's a good sign."

Anne frowned. "But then wouldn't that be the best time to see her?"

Stephen shook his head. "Her doctor felt she was coming to some conclusions that would be better left uninterrupted—especially by me."

"Maybe she still loves you."

Stephen laughed with grim amusement. "I rather doubt that's the case."

Anne thought for a while. "And if it were?" She covered her own keen interest with a light, chiding tone.

But Stephen smiled as though he'd caught her red-handed. "It wouldn't matter. She's like a sister to me at this point."

"I'm sorry," Anne offered politely.

"I'm not. We really weren't very good for each other." He sipped his wine pensively, seemingly caught in a moment's thought as he gazed into the amber-filled crystal.

Sensing he needed a moment of privacy, Anne sat back in her chair and watched the way the candle reflected its flame through her own glass. Even though Stephen showed no signs of unrequited love, she had the strongest sensation that he was harboring some assumed responsibility that remained very unresolved.

After some time had passed, Anne's eyes returned to Stephen. She'd expected him to be dwelling in that faraway corner of his mind, but she found him looking at her, again as though intrigued by something specific.

Slightly embarrassed, she tilted her head and smiled as she toyed with the rim of her glass. "Come on, Stephen, what is it?" she coaxed, feeling just comfortable enough to pursue it. "Is there something . . . wrong?"

Stephen's eyes dropped momentarily to the candle, and Anne could almost see the wheels spinning. Though he'd managed to avoid her detection the last time, she didn't see any way he could again. Yet within a second she saw a fleeting expression of mischief before it quickly disappeared. Next he seemed to ponder saying something but then reconsidered. Finally he shifted his weight forward as though to make a confession. By that time Anne's curiosity had mounted.

Stephen paused while a group from the next table gathered to leave, which made her lean even closer. "What *is* it?" she whispered.

His eyes darted to the left, then to the right before meeting hers pleadingly. "I have to go potty," he rasped. Stephen slowly bit his lip, looking gravely distressed.

Anne stared blankly into his eyes for a second, certain she'd misunderstood him. But amid all the rumors that had described "the roughly elegant Stephen Merrifield," there was one she'd totally forgotten. He was also known for an unpredictably bizarre sense of humor, and at the moment he was looking perfectly retarded.

"Oh, God," said Anne. She clapped a hand over her mouth to harness the uninhibited laughter that had always embarrassed her, but in the process she knocked her glass, spilling wine all over the crisp white linen. Then she was helpless.

Stephen tried to keep a straight face, but Anne's disruptive outburst had stopped every conversation in the tiny room. His repeated glances at her hopelessly contorted features finally forced the corners of his mouth to quiver.

Stephen reached across the table, dabbing roughly at her spilled wine with his napkin. "It's always refreshing to see a beautiful woman who can let herself go . . . just a tad."

That only made it worse, and a muscle began twitching in Stephen's chin as he waited for her to stop. "At least I'm not stuffy," he defended himself. Yet he was slowly blushing crimson, and he kept blotting mindlessly at the tablecloth as though that were the least he could do for her.

Finally, wiping away tears with a corner of her napkin, Anne shook her head in reproach. "You do . . . break right through the ice, I'll certainly say that."

The waiter arrived with a clean tablecloth and a calm, perfunctory smile, as though hysterical laughter and spilled wine were, after all, to be expected.

Stephen had the grace to wait until Anne looked reasonably back to normal before excusing himself. She watched as he walked toward the back room, and just before he rounded the corner, she caught his glance at her. He slowly shrugged as though the devil had made him do it. Then he disappeared.

By the time he returned, she'd been given a fresh glass of wine. She'd also suffered through the polite, excusing smiles of curious patrons, returning them as best she could.

"That wasn't fair," she accused.

"No, not fair at all," he admitted. "But it was effective."

"Now that's an understatement if I ever—" Suddenly Anne looked at him, her eyes squinting accusingly.

Stephen sat innocently across the table, but a slight smile of guilt peeked through. "I'll go to any end necessary sometimes." He laughed softly.

"Hmm. I'm beginning to see what they meant when they said you could be somewhat 'unorthodox' in finding ways out of things." Anne accepted defeat as Stephen picked up his menu. After all, the subject had once again been quite nicely averted, hadn't it?

Stephen's little joke had not only broken the ice, but also the serious tone of the conversation, and by midway through the evening couples at nearby tables were looking on at the oblivious pair with envy. As they chatted and laughed in a world of their own, nothing was even mentioned about unspoken rules in law firms.

By the time they left the restaurant, Anne had trouble remembering that life had existed prior to the past four hours. She'd never become so totally at ease so quickly with anyone else in her life.

As the little car slowly rounded the curves to Stephen's house, jet lag began to catch up with him. He settled back, seeming every bit as comfortable as she felt. Somehow all reality seemed to have faded into the distance.

Anne noted the unquestioned security that she felt in his presence, and after a while, she glanced at the massive body in the seat next to her. He'd drifted into a contented sleep, and she longed to curl up like a kitten against him.

As they pulled up to his street, Stephen took a deep breath on awakening. Pointing to his house, he remained in his reclining position as she came to a stop in his driveway.

She didn't know whether to turn her engine off or leave it on, so she left it on. Then, as though to answer her question for her, Stephen reached across the dashboard and turned the key before relaxing back against his seat. "Well, my fascinating little friend, here we are." He sighed.

Anne half smiled, but then she made an exaggerated pout. She didn't want the evening to end, ever.

"I know," he agreed, almost in a whisper. He looked as melancholy as she felt.

"What are you thinking *now*?" she asked, her voice wary.

Stephen said nothing for a moment, but then he leaned across the seat and slid his hand around the back of her neck. His lips covered hers in a caress so sweet and delicate that little tinkling bells seemed to ring from somewhere far off in her head.

The embrace was adoring, almost reverent, as though he were testing her lips to see just how they would fit. Yet under the surface of his unexpected tenderness, Anne could feel a suppressed hunger so wild that it left her breathless just from the hint of bridled passion.

Ignoring caution, Anne returned his kiss fully, almost daring him to release his response, but Stephen slowly pulled away from her lips. "That's part of what I've been thinking," he said softly.

At that moment all she wanted in the world was to dissolve herself into him, somehow joining him so that they would never be separated again. Never mind the fact that they'd just met—it didn't matter. Nothing mattered except that she didn't want to leave him.

Such a powerful feeling almost frightened her, and as though he'd read it, Stephen slowly placed a tiny kiss on her forehead, like an artist who'd just put the last brushstroke on a canvas. He gently blew aside a strand of hair from her face, but something in his eyes told her he was feeling exactly what she was feeling—yet understanding it no better than she did.

"Is this what all those cryptic little looks were about?"

"Partly," he whispered.

Anne's words seemed to come without volition. "I think . . . I'd like to know the rest." Her lips were parted in silent invitation.

Stephen smiled slowly, and he looked at her as if she were a child who'd said the most lovable thing he'd ever heard. "Don't tempt me," he commanded softly. Something in his voice told Anne to take the warning quite seriously.

Saying nothing more, Stephen gently pulled away from her and wrote his number on a pad of paper he found on the dash. "Call me when you get home so I won't worry about you."

He looked at her for a moment, appearing to search for words. Then, as though reconsidering, he simply sighed and shook his head before getting out of the car.

"Lock your door," he said, pushing down the button on his side before closing it. She watched as he walked in front of the car and into the house.

Anne drove the rest of the way home feeling as though she'd somehow been launched into another world. She'd spent no more than a concentrated five hours with someone she barely knew, yet there was absolutely no doubt in her mind: if there was any such thing as love at first sight, she felt she could now write volumes.

When Anne got home she went through her routine of checking every corner of the apartment. It seemed silly, but it was a habit her mother had instilled in her. The apartment was on the second floor, the only entrance in full view of other apartments in her complex. But Anne never felt quite at ease until she'd checked under her bed, in the shower and all the little closets and cupboards that could possibly house a human being of even the tiniest proportions.

After satisfying herself that she was alone, Anne called Stephen's number, carefully tucking the note in the back of her address book as his line rang.

She almost hung up, afraid she was rousing him from sleep when he answered drowsily.

"Did I wake you?"

"Um," he murmured. Anne could hear him roll over.

How would the tall, rugged man she'd met that day look sprawled in bed? "I almost didn't call you," she said.

"No, I'm glad you did," he protested. She could hear his sleepy breathing.

"Well," whispered Anne, "get a good night's rest."

For several minutes after they'd hung up Anne remained there, her hand lingering on the phone as though the instrument might have captured the dreamy warmth of him.

Little did she know as she fell into a trusting, contented slumber that Stephen would lie very much awake, trying to sort out thoughts from feelings. The thoughts were rational and familiar; the feelings, unexpected. But one thing was certain. They couldn't coexist.

3

OPENING ONE EYE long enough to see the clock on her bed-
stand, Anne decided to forgo the morning paper in order to
stay hidden from the world a little longer.

She closed her eyes again to maintain the hypnotic state,
but before long her thoughts wandered to the present. That
woke her up. She wanted to look perfect today.

Pushing a lock of hair away from her eyes, Anne made her
way out of bed and into the kitchen. "Coffee," she mumbled. "I want coffee! A serious task lies before me."

After a warm shower had made her feel human again,
Anne spent an hour dawdling with every detail until finally,
dressed in the taupe suit that matched her hair, she closed the
door to her apartment.

Leisurely driving over the winding canyon road, Anne
tried to anticipate if it would be uncomfortable seeing Stephen in the office. The thought of him in a business environ-
ment already seemed out of place. Instead, he should be
draped over the bar stool in her kitchen, sipping iced tea and
snitching a piece of carrot off the counter while she per-
formed great culinary magic.

As morning progressed slowly toward noon, Anne continued occupying herself with the minor incidents that creep
up in a law firm. She knew Stephen wouldn't be in until later,
but she stayed close to her office so she'd be there in case he
stopped by when he got back. Considering the odd note of
guilt in his voice when he'd discussed his ex-wife's unhappi-

ness, Anne wanted to be readily available in case he needed a devil's advocate. Or a shoulder, for that matter.

But by three-thirty she still hadn't heard from him, and she began to grow concerned for another reason. If he hadn't returned yet, she should start seeing about the status of his projects herself.

When Anne approached Stephen's area, his door was closed and Janet was typing busily. "Have you heard from Mr. Merrifield?"

Janet looked up. "He's in his office," she said, flipping her hair dramatically.

"Did he . . . just get here?"

"No, he's been here since noon," Janet answered offhandedly. "I've been waiting for another day like yesterday, but all he's given me is a list he said could probably stand retyping. Other than that I'm just killing time, so if you have anything else, I'm getting bored."

Anne looked at the page in the typewriter, and just about to answer, she stopped herself as Stephen's door opened.

He came out of his office looking harassed. "Hello, Anne." His tone of voice was just strained enough to ring an offkey bell, and Anne felt unsettled by it for a moment. But then she could hardly expect a warmer greeting in front of one of the secretaries.

"I didn't know if you'd returned, so I thought I'd better stop by and see if I should follow up on anything."

"Thanks, but everything's in control," he answered. Yet something in his eyes told her it was a lie.

Suddenly Anne's thoughts went to Cathy, his ex-wife. "Did your meeting this morning go all right?" She was hoping he'd take the opportunity to invite her into his office under the pretext of discussing the meeting, but just then she saw that one of the other partners was inside.

"It went fine," said Stephen, dismissing her erroneous guess. "I'm locked into meetings all afternoon," he added. He looked as if he desperately wanted to talk to her but was prevented by a door that had somehow closed between them. Anne neither liked nor understood the barrier.

Suddenly she heard a voice boom from inside Stephen's office. "Tom! Well, for once we have a good connection—the fish must be sleeping!" Then, more loudly, "Stephen! I finally got through! Hold on, Tom. Janet! Find Merrifield, I have Japan on the line!"

Stephen shrugged in helpless disgust before stepping through the doorway and disappearing around the corner.

What in the world? thought Anne, trying to make sense of the odd communication she'd just received. Suddenly she felt Janet staring at her, and she realized how long she'd been standing there, still looking blankly at the corner Stephen had rounded.

Quickly catching herself, Anne glanced at her watch. With only a little more than an hour of the working day left, there was little point in assigning Janet any overload. Besides, Anne thought, heading back toward her office, she had more to think about than an hour of Janet's time.

The rest of the workday passed with Anne glued to her office, but Stephen neither called nor stopped by. Finally at five o'clock, she made her rounds throughout the suite to be certain no last-minute overtime arrangements had to be made. As she passed Stephen's office she noted that his door was still closed.

"Oh, how convenient," said Janet as she held out a plain white envelope along with her time slip for Anne to sign. "I was just on my way to your office—you saved me the trouble."

Terrific, thought Anne. She took the time sheet, and as she reviewed the entries, her eyes fell on the envelope that she'd turned over in her hand. It was addressed to her by the same pen that had written, "Call S. Merrif—" the day before, and it had the familiar inscription, "personal and confidential," in the lower left-hand corner.

As her signature dug into the thin triplicate of the time sheet, Anne asked if Stephen had left for the day, keeping her tone light and uninterested.

"No, he hasn't. He's been in his office with his partners all afternoon, running up phone bills to Japan as though they were talking to Orange County. He hasn't even surfaced, so I asked him at ten to five if he wanted me to stay, and he told me to go. He certainly can be abrupt," she complained.

Anne brightened as she walked Janet toward the reception room. Obviously that was the answer. With Stephen's schedule, he was running on all fours! No wonder he'd looked so strained.

After seeing Janet out the door, Anne returned to her office. She was dying to read the note, just certain it would ask her to meet him somewhere after hours. But it was less than what she'd hoped for by a long shot.

Circe—I'd rather have talked, but I'm locked in here and not alone.

It was a gift to spend time with an angel. At first I told myself it would merely be a pleasant end to a tired day, but then she sang, and I knew it carried the sure promise of deafening my ears to my own good sense, which had already shown definite signs of slipping. I have to use prudence while it's still available, so given "the circumstances," please accept my apology—to us both. I hope you can understand.

Stephen

Anne stared at the words on the page as though they'd been

written in another language. She didn't understand them, yet the message was clear. Stephen was backing away.

Her eyes returned to the note. Its general tone was definitely without insult, but it was also, unmistakably, final. Reflecting on the way Stephen had looked when she'd talked to him just an hour earlier, she tried to put a tag on his expression. Disgusted? Actually, it had been more like "resolved."

Anne sat in her office for some time, unable to draw anything but a massive blank. Finally she tried to tell herself it didn't matter—she'd only known the man for twenty-four hours, and she'd been unusually attracted to him, that was all. No more, no less.

But in the very next second she was through fooling herself, because it did matter. She'd spent time with an angel, as well, and she didn't want him to just fly away without a better explanation than that. The rapport between them had been too natural to let it go without at least an attempt to investigate what had happened. *Who knows,* she thought, *maybe he's misinterpreted something. That's the problem with falling in love with someone you don't know.* Then she caught herself. *Falling in love? In less than twenty-four hours? That's ridiculous.*

Anne folded the note and walked down the empty hallway toward the litigation side of the office. On the rare chance that all the meetings had broken up and Stephen was alone, she just might muster the courage to stop in.

Instead she met with a surprise. The door was open, the lights were out and his briefcase was gone.

Anne stood there a moment, staring into the darkened room. She felt stunned, she felt angry and she felt cheated. Yet the worst part of it was that she wasn't quite sure she had a right to feel anything at all.

With the halls quiet by then, Anne walked slowly into Stephen's empty office. There was the faintest trace of the scent she'd inhaled throughout the previous evening, and her thoughts focused on that brief moment in his arms, when she had wanted to dissolve herself into the deliciousness of him and never surface.

But now things were clearly quite different, and the taunting scent seemed to mock her.

Enough of this, she thought, wanting to challenge Stephen's effect on her. She crossed the room, stopping at his desk. There was absolute silence in the halls.

Knowing she was alone, Anne rounded the path to his side of the desk. She slowly lowered herself into his chair, sinking into the richly upholstered tweed that still held the warmth of his essence.

Her eyes fell to his desk pad, and amid some quickly jotted computations, there was a drawing of a heart inside a cube. That was an odd combination. She studied it more closely.

The heart had been painstakingly shaded so that it had almost a three-dimensional life of its own, yet the cube looked as though made of transparent steel.

The diagram could be taken in as many different ways as the note she still held in her hand; each was equally cryptic. As she looked at the drawing, a flash of perverse humor made her consider drawing an egg around the doodle. But she resisted it, if for no other reason than that she didn't want to admit she'd gone into his office.

Finally, having risen to leave, Anne noticed the dense silence as she walked slowly back to her office. It was eerily quiet. Even after hours there was usually someone working late, but Friday night was occasionally an exception. Tonight even Mr. Tomlin's workaholic area was still.

Anne returned to her office to collect her things. Each little movement she made seemed to echo into the hallway. She picked up the fresh-up kit she'd packed in case Stephen asked her out to dinner, and suddenly the quietness seemed deathly. She was going to have to put this whole thing into some kind of perspective, because at the moment all she could consistently feel was a stinging confusion.

Heading her car west on Wilshire Boulevard, Anne immediately dreaded getting on the freeway to sit in the long, slow climb of traffic over the hill. She considered taking the canyon route instead—at least it was more scenic. *Besides, you fall off a horse, you get back on, right?* She turned toward Beverly Glen.

As the car rounded the curve by the little store, Anne's mood sank again. Why hadn't he said . . . *something*? She could only look back on hours that were too perfect to end with such a baffling departure.

Maybe he had just considered last night a casual dinner with a co-worker. Maybe she'd imagined the special rapport she'd thought they'd both felt. Or maybe she'd made more of it than there had been. On the other hand, a man didn't usually give a casual co-worker the kiss she remembered. Yet she had to admit he'd been the one to end the embrace. Twice.

THE WEEKEND BEGAN. Each hour threatened to pass more slowly than the last, so Saturday morning Anne became determined to keep herself busy around the apartment. She cleaned every corner, running up and down the stairs to the laundry room, sweeping the porch, even sweeping the outside stairs. She tried not to think of Stephen, continuously reminding herself that she had no real right to expect anything from him. But his image loomed persistently behind every thought.

Finally the apartment was spotless. With her windows sparkling in the sunlight, Anne glanced at her watch. It was only eleven-fifty. Disgusted, she wiped her forehead with the sleeve of her faded red workshirt and plunked herself down on the sofa.

Suddenly the idea crossed her mind to just get in the car. Go for a drive. Maybe a change of scenery would put things in perspective, because this mood was trying to lock its own door.

Following her instincts, Anne stopped long enough to grab her purse and a pair of rubber thongs, and within ten minutes she was driving toward the ocean. She'd come back without this gloom if it took the whole day.

Three hours later, when the little white Nissan pulled back into its own carport, Anne glanced at herself in the rearview mirror. "Mission accomplished," she said.

The engine had no sooner come to an abrupt stop then Anne was out of the car, heading straight for the stairway. She left the keys in the front door, not even bothering to close it as she swept into the kitchen to pour a fast cup of the coffee that was now mud. She didn't care—the black, soupy liquid only reminded her of how clear and crisp her mood had become by contrast.

The drive, the sea air and the two-mile walk on the beach had all served to purge that horrid blue funk. Not only that, but they had also paved the way for some rather brilliant conclusions on the way home, if she did say so herself. The answer was so clear! Why hadn't she seen it hours ago?

This whole silly infatuation with Merrifield had been nothing more than a typical Anne-like ploy to avoid dealing with what really mattered—her career and K&W's failure to come through quite the way she'd expected. What else could possibly explain such an intense reaction to someone she'd just met?

Now that she saw it, it made perfect sense, knowing herself as she did. Here she'd been, sitting passively by, waiting for K&W to hand her some death-defying responsibility on a silver platter. The simple truth of the matter was that she'd felt intimidated by K&W from the first day she'd stepped out of the elevator, and she'd done nothing but hide in the safety of her office ever since.

Then, just when she was starting to get concerned, along came Merrifield. And instead of meeting the K&W problem head-on, she'd glommed onto a convenient opportunity to stay oblivious just a little longer. After all, who can be expected to function when her brain has been pickled by raging horomones? And who could pickle them more easily than someone like Stephen Merrifield? Anne was no fool. If she needed a diversion, she chose a good one.

Well, the tendency to play fat, dumb and happy ostrich was one side of herself she'd gotten used to. But the ability to take action was another—once she recognized the ostrich burying its ugly little head, that is. Ah, life could be so easy if you just opened your eyes.

Going to the phone, Anne dialed Trudy's number in Oregon, praying her friend would be home. She didn't want any mindless detail watering down the mood she'd mustered up. It felt too good.

"What a surprise!" shouted Trudy. Anne could hear the blaring of a television set until Trudy had the same thought and turned it down.

"Well, things must be going well," Trudy said. "I haven't heard from you, so they must be keeping you busy."

"Yes, well, I want to talk to you about that, but first things first—how's your back?"

"Oh, I'm so sick of hanging in odd positions that I can't believe it. They're finally deciding to do the damned surgery, and I can't wait. Get it on, I've begged them but they're so conservative about back surgery it's ridiculous."

Anne laughed. "So how does it feel to be back in Oregon?"

"Oh, Anne." She beamed. "If you ever came here to visit you'd never go back to that smoke pot. It's wonderful! You'd be surprised how many of my old friends have come to visit. I was afraid they'd all be boring by now, but they're actually pretty up on things.

"Oh!" Trudy continued, "It's so good to be here, I can't tell you—K&W seems a world away. Speaking of the devil, how's it going for you?"

Anne carried the phone to the couch, dragging the neatly wrapped cord out of its coils. "I need some advice, Trudy."

"Oh? Are they giving you stuff you can't handle?"

Anne laughed. "Don't I wish that were the problem—I'd be in seventh heaven. No, I'm afraid it's worse than that. They've given me absolutely nothing to do instead."

"You're kidding."

"Nope, I'm not. Maybe they think I can't handle it or something, but no one's asked for a thing beyond the scope of overtime or temps. I've been feeling absolutely useless."

"Gee. When I talked to Tomlin after the arrangements had been made, I told him you were great in personnel and that he should take advantage of letting you set things up while I'm gone. He said he would, so I don't understand that at all."

Anne thought about Tomlin's one-hundred-fifty page complaint and the team of crazed people who'd continuously buzzed around his office. "Well, maybe that's part of it," she conceded. "The day I started, he got the word to file some antitrust action, and there was a time pressure on it—"

"General Consolidated?"

"Yes. He's had upwards of six attorneys on it all the time, and it's been like watching a small, separate law firm do their own thing. They don't even say hello—they just run around with furrowed brows, poring over reams of paper."

"Well, there's the problem, I'd suspect. If Tomlin's gotten the go-ahead on bringing that action, it's a really complicated matter, and— When will it be filed?"

"Yesterday," said Anne.

"Oh, well give it another week," Trudy suggested, sounding relieved. "And as far as the day-to-day stuff is concerned, hell—each of the original seed firms ran pretty smoothly, and they're used to being self-sufficient, so you might not get a lot of requests to wipe runny noses. But maybe now that Tomlin's complaint has been filed—"

"Trudy, how long has he been managing partner?"

"Oh, it's only been a couple of months now."

Anne continued with her thought. "Did you find him . . . difficult?"

Trudy laughed. "Naw," she said. "Most of my dealings have been with Cooper, and I don't know Tomlin very well, but my impression is that he's a sweetheart underneath it all—don't let him throw ya."

"Well, what would you think if I were to just approach him and tell him straight out that I'm bored to death."

Trudy giggled. "He'd love it! No one ever 'tells' him anything. They ask. He'd probably find it refreshing as hell."

"Hmm. Well, maybe I'll just do that little thing."

"Sure! What have you got to lose?"

Anne winced slightly at the familiar sound of that question. She'd played it back to herself a hundred times, and even though it sounded reasonable, there had been moments she'd begun to wonder if Trudy didn't take life just a little too casually from time to time.

"So what else is new?" Trudy certainly sounded chipper.

"Well, not much," said Anne, wondering whether she should mention Stephen. Why not, she thought. She was still going to have to run into him in the hallways on a daily basis, and it wouldn't hurt to get some insight into his psyche. After all, he was still a K&W partner she'd be dealing with. "Merrifield came back to town for two days, and—"

"Ooh," Trudy breathed heavily into the phone. "Isn't he the most *gorgeous* hunk you've ever laid eyes on?"

Anne laughed at Trudy's enthusiasm. "He's not without merit," she agreed, keeping her voice light. At least she wasn't the only one. "What do you know about him?"

"A-ha! I knew he'd blow your mind once you saw him. Well, put him out of your mind, my dear."

"Oh? What do you mean?" This could be interesting. At least Trudy might say something that would make her feel a little better about the note.

"He'd just never get involved with someone in the firm, that's all. I'm not sure he gets involved with anyone, for that matter. He seems to keep himself inundated with work, and—hmm." Trudy interrupted herself. "Why did you ask . . . like that?"

Anne could picture the coy little smile Trudy so often displayed. "Oh, no reason. I had dinner with him Thursday night, and—"

"You what?" Trudy gasped.

"It was nothing," Anne explained. "He came directly to the office from the airport and didn't have his car, so I drove him home. On the way he asked if I wanted to have dinner with him, so—"

"He asked you?"

"Good heavens." Anne started to laugh. "Well, I didn't ask him!"

"Anne, you haven't told anyone in the firm about it, have you?"

"Of course not. But why are you so shocked?"

"Oh! Well!" Trudy switched into her gossip mode. "That's the biggie at K&W. Even more than usual, there's this huge understanding written in gigantic red letters: *Thou shalt not dip thy pen in company ink!* Oh, God! I just can't believe it!" She giggled. "And Merrifield, of all people!"

Of all people? Now Anne was curious. "Why do you say that?"

"Oh, because he's so damned visible! He's their very own shining star—absolutely brilliant! The big Example, writ large! He wasn't part of either half before the merger, but they made him such a good offer that he left his own firm, of which he was a senior partner. And get this! Out of loyalty to his old partners, he refused to take even one case with him. And K&W took him, anyway! Yes, he's noticed, all right!"

Well, at least Anne didn't have to wonder if she'd personally done something to turn him off.

Trudy went on in the same vein. "God! I just can't imagine a partner going against that little rule—they're all so paranoid about it after what happened last year that they won't even employ husband and wife teams."

Then, realizing that Anne didn't know what she was talking about, Trudy explained. "When the merger first came together, K&W lost an incredibly valuable partner. He left his wife for one of the other lawyers, and—oh, Anne! It was just an awful mess. There was so much disruption and flack about it that at this point all the attorneys—associates, as well—keep a good ten-foot distance from anything in a dress. But especially Merrifield. He gets so many subliminal . . . offers, if you will."

"Well, maybe he thinks I'm a boy," Anne said, looking at the sand under her nails. Switching the phone to her other hand, she reached over the armrest of the couch, expecting to find the nail file. But she'd put it away.

"Who could think you're a boy." Trudy laughed. "Oh, God, I can just see the two of you together. Did he . . . did you . . ." The verbal bumbling gave Anne the rest of the sentence.

"No, of course not. We just had dinner, that's all. He's returning to Philadelphia sometime over the weekend. No more, no less than that."

"When does he come back?"

"Sometime next week—Thursday or Friday, I think." There was a tiny pebble lodged under her nail, and Anne propped herself up to look on the end table. Stephen's note was protruding from under a magazine, and she cradled the phone between her ear and shoulder, using a folded corner to dig out the pebble.

"Well, I'm truly amazed," continued Trudy. "Are you going to see him again?"

"Nope." Anne's answer was simple but definite. She absentmindedly unfolded the note, her eyes skimming over Stephen's handwriting.

"Well, you must have really made an impression, I'll say that for you. Merrifield's so used to being fawned over that he pays absolutely no attention to the women there. In fact, he's almost downright rude."

"Yes, well, maybe that's the easiest way," replied Anne, suddenly preoccupied by a word she somehow hadn't noticed before.

"Did he . . . kiss you, at least?" Trudy was coming unglued on the other end of the phone.

"Uh, well, in a way," said Anne. She focused on the first word again, amazed that she hadn't noticed it on first reading.

"'In a way,' she says! *Oh, swoon!*" hollered Trudy. "Anne, that man has always been such a mystery to me! He's such a fox that you'd think he'd be a real player. Cooper's tried to fix him up with his niece, who's supposed to be God's gift to mankind, by the way, but he just begs off politely."

"Yep, that's a mystery, all right," agreed Anne, keeping her tone light. "Speaking of mysteries, Trudy would you refresh my memory? Who was Circe again?"

"God, woman, where's your mythology?" Trudy teased. "You remember old Circe. She's the beautiful goddess who dwells on an island, and if a sailor gets too close he hears her singing and becomes enraptured, at which point Circe changes him into a beast. And the sailor crashes into the rocks, shipwrecked. Why?"

4

MONDAY MORNING Anne was at her desk at eight o'clock, although the office didn't open until nine.

Up until now she hadn't felt comfortable moving anything in Trudy's office or even rearranging the contents of her desk. As in other matters, she'd idly waited for the firm to get her involved. But this was a new day all the way around. She started with the top right-hand drawer.

If at K&W she made mistakes, then she made mistakes, dammit. But she wasn't going to be a passive bystander.

As for Stephen, he somehow kept popping out of the little corner of her brain that she'd reserved just for him on the way home from the beach. Even more so once she'd confirmed what Circe meant. But she'd already decided not to make too much of that part. He was probably just trying to make the note easier to swallow.

By the time people started arriving everything in Trudy's office had been rearranged, with unwanted items packed into a box in case she did change her mind about coming back. But until that happened, Anne decided, she was damned well going to stop thinking of it as "Trudy's office."

Glancing at her watch, Anne found her nerve and called Tomlin to ask if she could come see him.

"I'm glad you called, Anne. I was going to call you, as a matter of fact. Stephen Merrifield told me how you flew into action, getting him lined up with a little cadre of workers at the last minute—and without disturbing my resources," he added delightedly.

"So now that my cumbersome antitrust complaint has been filed safely with the court clerk, I'd very much like to get you started on some projects. And now would be an excellent time."

A few minutes later Anne walked in and took the seat across from Mr. Tomlin. Setting a pad of paper on her side of his desk, she simply waited.

Tomlin was a lean, meticulously groomed little fellow who had the capacity for instilling terror in the staff. He tolerated no avoidable mistakes, expecting people to think about what they were doing. A slipup resulting from carelessness or inattentiveness brought a reprimand that had been known to reduce a secretary to tears. But as long as everyone "functioned intelligently," meaning they did everything right, he was as gentle as a lamb.

"You'll have to forgive me, my dear," Tomlin began, "but Trudy's departure happened rather quickly, and I've forgotten... Didn't she say you excelled in personnel matters?" His eyes were hawklike, as though looking for some sign of nervousness, but that was all she needed to show none.

In less than an hour Anne walked out of his office with more than she'd hoped for—a book jammed with assignments and a whole new perspective on the feared Mr. Tomlin. After all, anyone who used corny euphemisms like "tightening the ship without rocking the boat" couldn't be all that threatening. Especially when he chuckled about them, as though the phrases were too horrid even for him.

The work he assigned was right down Anne's alley. An initial analysis of out-of-date policy and benefits, along with trying to negotiate a good deal on dictating machines. Anne had been wondering how they'd gotten along, with half the firm using the minis they'd brought in with the merger, and the other half using standards. But Tomlin's week-long search for overload secretaries with the right size transcribers had finally put him at the end of his rope.

Anne began by superficially checking every direction at once, and within a few hours things began to feel normal. Her phone started ringing off the hook with call-backs, and in the middle of it all one of the secretaries called in tears to give notice.

No sooner had Maria hung up than her boss called to announce the resignation. The dreaded Ron Lessinger, known for his impossible demands, wanted Anne in his office immediately. It never rains, she thought on her way across the suite.

"Tell me," Anne finally said after ten minutes of complaints about Maria, "what's your idea of the perfect secretary? It'll give me an idea of what to look for," she encouraged.

Lessinger's eyes gleamed. "Someone with a brain," he began. "And preferably no children." Then he proceeded to list all the traits that could never come all in the same person.

Well, at least this firm had some typical litigators, Anne thought as she left his office. At least she knew how to deal with those.

DURING THE NEXT FEW DAYS life consisted of switching gears from interviewing to negotiating with dictating machine sales reps to delving into another phase of policy and then back to interviewing secretaries.

In the middle of the last scheduled interview, Tomlin called and asked her to prepare a billing report including the recent billing rate increases. Mr. Cooper wanted it for the partners' meeting Monday night.

On an odd premonition, Anne interrupted the interview and buzzed the computer room. Even though there was plenty of time, she told Ralph she needed the report on a rush basis.

An hour later Ralph confirmed that it had been an uncanny intuition, because the computer kept spitting out the accounts receivable ledger. The whole section that counted billable hours seemed to be missing. After explaining that he'd been working out some other bugs, Ralph thought it may have gotten hidden. The question was, where?

Anne decided to stay late. While Ralph was working with the software, maybe she could recognize the figures in other runs, just by chance.

As everyone was leaving for the day, Anne took a huge stack of runs and began poring over them while she walked slowly down the hall toward her office. She took the shortcut through the reception room and, as she opened the door, someone was just coming through from the opposite direction.

Anne was so engrossed in her search that without bothering to look up she stepped aside and waited for the other person to pass. But no one moved.

"After you," said Stephen belatedly. His voice was totally calm, but Anne's heart dropped.

Time seemed to freeze as eyes met openly. In his she could read understanding somehow mixed with a solemn apology. But Anne was more concerned about what might be showing in hers, because she was totally unprepared for the way she was now feeling—paralyzed.

"Oh, I'm sorry," she said a little too lightly as she motioned to her papers. Yet she noticed her hand was shaking ever so slightly. Why was she feeling like this? Where were all those rational thoughts?

Anne immediately tried to cover the catch she'd heard in her voice. "I didn't realize you were waiting for me, as well."

Stephen said nothing, but one eyebrow slowly raised as though she'd said something ironic.

Frantically searching for some way to end the encounter, Anne's eyes dropped to the boxful of files he was holding. "Good heavens!" She laughed. "No wonder you couldn't get through—here, let me get the door for you." She was doing an excellent job, if she thought so herself.

"Thank you," he said, maneuvering himself and the box past her. Anne kept her eyes safely on the large carton, but her peripheral vision told her that Stephen's were very much on her.

Though she was careful to give him a wide berth, it was impossible for his arm not to brush against her as he passed. The contact of their skin was all it took to send an electrical impulse to her brain. Compounding that was the familiar, heady scent that now had Stephen's name on it.

Not trusting what her eyes might betray, the second he was through the doorway Anne disappeared into the reception room to safety. Her heart fluttered like the wings of a bird in first flight, and her fingers were trembling, try as she might to contain her reaction.

Come on, Anne, it's just the surprise of no warning, she told herself. But the flustered feeling lingered, telling her something else.

Anne had a difficult time concentrating after that, and she went home feeling rattled, if not downright defeated. *Damn.* He looked ten times more desirable than he had before. She was enraged with herself for still finding him so lethally attractive after she'd already rationalized that he'd really represented nothing more than a passing distraction.

But there it was—the same feeling she'd had from the first moment she'd seen him. Only now it seemed even stronger. She knew it wasn't going to go away a second time.

Get him out of your mind, Anne kept repeating to herself. But it sure would have been easier had she not seen that haunting warmth in his eyes.

Anne had a few more visual encounters with Stephen on Thursday and Friday, but she couldn't read what was on his face. She'd have preferred to see a blank expression, but instead there had been something like an unanswered question. She willed herself to stay objective, but each time she saw him her heart skipped a beat. Her mind seemed to scramble.

Wanting to avoid him as best she could, Anne stayed in her office as much as possible. Luckily there were constant telephone calls, since she was volleying with dictating machine reps and negotiating the offer Lessinger wanted to extend to the first secretary Anne had interviewed.

So that's the answer, Anne decided as Friday neared an end. *Just stay busy and ignore him. So what if he turns you into a bowl of Jell-O. Just live with the feeling until it dissipates. It can't stay this strong if you don't feed it. Nothing does.*

Just when Anne was beginning to panic, Ralph called with the news that he'd finally found the billable hours that the computer had misplaced. There was still a problem with the billing rates, but he'd be in the office on Sunday, and he'd work on it then. If there was any difficulty, he'd notify her.

SUNDAY AFTERNOON RALPH CALLED. There had been a bug in the program, he explained, and the billing rates were "relatively" correct but not "actually."

"What do you mean, 'relatively' correct, Ralph?" Anne was almost afraid to hear the answer.

"Well, they're wrong but consistently wrong." He laughed, obviously enjoying her confusion. "Don't worry, though, I'm working out a conversion chart. The billing rates aren't accurate as they show on the run itself, but by applying the conversion chart to what you see on the computer run, you'll be able to get your correct figures."

Anne pulled the phone cord loose from under the radio. "It sounds horrible."

"No, not bad. You'll have to make two calculations, though—one for before March and one for after. Plus, the billing rates of some of the attorneys raised more than others, so it's not a linear conversion."

She plunked down on the couch with a groan. "Now it sounds worse than horrible."

"Well, if there's any way you can stop in this afternoon, I'll be here till five, and I can explain it to you. It's really not that complicated once you understand it."

"Neither is Einstein's theory—once you understand it."

He laughed at the dread in her voice. "Trust me. Twenty minutes on a Sunday afternoon will make it yours forever."

Anne laughed. "Gee, that sounds kind of sexy, Ralph."

He paused. "Oh, no, you don't!" She could almost see his hands thrust onto his hips. "Just because my warm, sweet body is in here alone, don't think you can come in and molest it, because I'm saving myself, dearie."

"Oh, well, I gave it a good try." Anne yawned. "I'd like to come down as early as possible, though. When will you be through putting together your conversion chart?"

"I can have it for you by four o'clock."

"Okay, I'll be there at four."

When Anne arrived Ralph was undoing another kink that had surfaced when he'd untangled the accrued time records. He poured a cup of coffee for each of them and set about explaining how to use the chart. It was simple enough, but it involved several steps.

Just to be sure she understood, Anne explained it back to him and then plugged a few sample attorneys' times and rates into her calculator. It all came out accurately.

"Amazing!" she exclaimed. "Ralph, you're brilliant!"

Anne went into the Xerox room to make copies, since there was no competition for the machines. She stopped by her office to drop them off, and just for the fun of it, tried the conversion chart on a few more time and rate combinations. She wanted to be absolutely sure before getting too far from Ralph, since he wasn't coming in on Monday.

Absorbed in the conversion steps, Anne didn't hear anyone approach. She jumped at the sound of Stephen's voice.

"Well, from the looks of things this week, at least you're no longer bored." He was standing in her doorway, dressed in tan slacks and a light blue sport shirt open at the neck. He looked gorgeous.

In spite of the pounding of her own heart, Anne looked at him as casually as she could. "No, bored I'm not, thank God. I was about to climb a tree before this." She returned to her computer run. "And when I get bored I'll do just about anything to relieve it," she added.

"Touché," he said. The comment was delivered in a way that told her nothing, yet there was a softness in his voice that she hadn't counted on hearing.

Why wasn't he just ignoring her the way she wanted to ignore him, she wondered. "Did you finish your depositions?"

"Yes, for the time being," he said. "Do you mind if I come in?"

Anne hesitated, wishing she felt more in control, but without waiting for her reply, Stephen entered the room and lowered himself into the chair across from her desk. He folded his arms and crossed his legs. For a long moment he looked her directly in the eye.

"I assume you got my note."

Anne felt her veneer of indifference dissolve under his patient scrutiny, and she laughed slightly, her eyes still on the computer run. "What there was of it—I wasn't quite sure I understood all of its ramifications, but the general gist was clear." She lifted her eyes to meet his sincere directness. It seemed silly to do otherwise.

Stephen paused for a moment, appraising her mood, but then he appeared to disregard it.

"I'd like to have a talk." It wasn't a request but rather an announcement.

Anne looked at him for a moment, amazed at how easily he cut right through her defenses. Yet she wasn't angry, and her voice sounded natural. "'Under the circumstances,' Stephen, I don't think that would be a good idea." She stressed the first three words, quoting his own note.

His eyes were soft but at the same time steadfast, as though he found her resistance perfectly understandable. "'Under the circumstances,' Anne, I think it would be a particularly good idea."

Stephen glanced toward the doorway of Anne's office, although she knew no one was around. "Let's take a drive, shall we?"

Based on what Trudy had said about his being so visible, it seemed like a reasonable request. The only question was, did Anne want to expose herself to further contact with him? She didn't want to put any more chinks in her armor. It was already dangerously flimsy.

"Stephen, I really don't know if I'd be very good at addressing much of anything with you beyond a computer run at the moment." Hearing the tone in her own voice, Anne was surprised to realize that she hadn't bothered to hide her vulnerability. Another chink.

Stephen's voice was softly encouraging as he rose to his feet. "I'll do the talking." He walked to the door.

His expression indicated she'd be safe enough, and she began to feel a little foolish. Maybe he just wanted to apologize or something. After all, it was clearly necessity rather than preference that had convinced him to deliver his opinion in a note. Besides, as perceptive as he was, he had undoubtedly read right through all her feeble attempts to look impervious to him. So maybe letting him say his piece would let her end her own little song and dance on the note of a friendly handshake.

"Come on," he coaxed, standing in the doorway.

Anne took a resigned breath and let the computer run fall with a smack onto her desk. "Sure. Why not." But her voice had the tone of someone who had finally seen the logic of having all her teeth pulled out.

TEN MINUTES LATER the pungent smell of leather enveloped Anne as she sank into the rich, naturally tanned seat. Five seconds more, and the engine purred its way to noiseless efficiency.

Stephen said nothing but turned west on Wilshire with purpose, as though he were heading for a specific destination. Somehow there was an unspoken agreement to defer all discussion until they reached it. It seemed rather ludicrous to discuss the clouding weather, so Anne decided to just sit back, collect her thoughts and enjoy the ride.

She might have guessed he'd have a custom-appointed Lincoln rather than something more flashy like a Porsche or a Corvette. The panther-black elegance matched Stephen's understated power.

As he made a right turn onto Pacific Coast Highway, Anne looked at him for a brief, questioning moment. There was virtually nothing between where they were and the fashionable, residential beach community of Malibu. But his nod merely said, "Have patience."

Anne settled back in her seat, her head against the cushiony headrest. She closed out all but her own thoughts and the smell of cowhide that surrounded her. A click brought music from nowhere in particular, yet it filled the car.

After a while Anne parted her lids ever so slightly to sneak an appraising glance at Stephen. He was lost in his own thoughts, his left elbow on his knee as he unconsciously stroked his chin.

Anne studied the masculine line of his jaw. What would it be like to live in a body as powerful as his? He looked so virile, his ruddy complexion meeting healthy rich brown hair.

A sudden smile played at the corner of Anne's mouth as she noticed for the first time that his hair had thinned slightly on top. Ah! A flaw. Somehow it made her feel better.

Anne's eyes fell to Stephen's arm, partially exposed by his rolled-up sleeve. She focused on the soft, even blanket of dark brown hair. *I wonder what it would be like to stroke my cheek against that arm?* she pondered leisurely. She could almost feel the velvety thickness as she imagined it against her lips.

Realizing where her thoughts were heading, Anne closed her eyes once more, not wanting to torture herself with the compelling attraction she was trying so desperately to ignore. After all, this conversation was to be a peace talk. *Don't weaken the armor any more, Anne.*

Anne directed her thoughts to the forthcoming conversation. *I'll just be reasonable. I'll listen to what he has to say. I'll tell him I understand, and I'll agree that it was a wonderful evening, but that because of the "circumstances," we shouldn't have had dinner together in the first place. I'll assure him that I respect the position he's in, that I don't hold anything against him and that I'm perfectly capable of working in the same office without shooting him meaningful looks at every turn.*

As much as Anne hadn't wanted to open up the subject, when it came right down to it she could well understand Stephen's needing to assure himself that he hadn't handled the matter poorly. In fact, she quite respected him for having the determination to address it.

Alerted by the gradual slowing of the car, Anne opened her eyes to see where they were. The blinker signaled a left turn, which put them on a badly paved road.

As the car rocked its way slowly toward a turnoff overlooking the sea, Anne saw another little dirt road, which led to a lovely cliff site under a tree. There was an unobstructed view of the ocean from there and miles of sweeping coastline. *At least he likes serene settings,* she thought.

Finally the car came to a stop, and Stephen turned off the engine. Then there was absolute silence. The push of a button lowered both their windows, and a soft sea breeze brought in the faint scent of the ocean. With the same deliberation, Stephen reached toward the dash, silencing the radio.

Anne kept her eyes fixed straight ahead. The only sound now was the steady, faraway crashing of the waves below them. And inside the car, the rhythmical pounding of her heart.

Then came the creaking of leather along with the calm, deep breath Stephen took as he adjusted himself into a comfortable sideways position so he could look at her.

With her peripheral vision Anne watched him place his left elbow on the steering wheel and his right on the back of his seat. He formed his index fingers into a steeple in front of his lips, and then he sat there for a long moment. When he finally spoke, his voice was intimate yet direct.

"Anne, something very odd happened to me the night you and I had dinner."

Suddenly she wanted to make it as easy for him as she could, and she met his eyes openly.

"On a compulsion, I asked you to dinner because you represented a refreshing break from antitrust depositions and crazy ex-wives. I told myself we'd just stop and have a light dinner with light conversation. Then you'd drop me off, and that would be that."

Anne smiled sympathetically, her voice softly coaxing. "And that's really all that happened. I understand."

Stephen slowly shook his head. "That isn't all that happened."

Anne realized how transparent she must have been, and she looked out over the ocean. "Well, except for a little kiss—" She gestured with her hand to indicate that she hadn't found anything too wrong about it.

Stephen took another deep breath. "It wasn't just 'a little kiss,'" he said quietly. "And the kiss is only part of what I'm talking about."

Anne silenced herself. Just how transparent had she been?

"When I went into the house, I felt like I'd opened a Pandora's box, and all I knew was that I had to close it quickly."

He certainly was perceptive. That's exactly what it had felt like. A Pandora's box. "Well, your note was appropriate, then."

"This doesn't make a lot of sense," he continued, "but something just clicked in my mind the first moment I saw you. I guess I had to pursue it to see where it led."

"So? You defied all convention and asked someone in the firm to dinner," she supplied.

"That's right."

"And when you got into the house and back to your . . . senses, you realized you shouldn't have. I work at K&W, and that's not acceptable behavior for a partner."

"That's exactly right," he confirmed.

"Gee, Stephen, that's quite a serious problem." Anne tried to offer him a playful smile of understanding, hoping to make this a little easier for both of them. But what she found were warm, brown eyes that seemed to see way too much.

Stephen closed his eyes for a second and then looked at her once more. *Here comes the apology,* she thought.

"No, the problem came when I became intoxicated by sheer beauty, acute intelligence and this thing I can't quite define. So I took it a little further and kissed you."

Anne looked at him, wishing he didn't need to dwell on every detail. "Stephen, please don't feel that you've done anything wrong. I understand, really I do."

"And then I wrote a tidy little note and returned to Philadelphia, knowing that by the time I got back, everything would be in perspective."

She nodded, assuring him it had happened just like that.

Stephen slowly shook his head. "No, Anne. Try though I might, I haven't succeeded in getting you out of my mind."

Everything seemed to stop as Anne realized what she'd just heard. She'd been so caught up in her own scenario that she hadn't really listened to anything he'd said. She had just been waiting for him to get it over with.

She turned toward him, her eyes evaluating him. This time she said nothing.

"When I ran into you in the reception room, I could see the sign on your forehead: Headed West, Do Not Disturb." Stephen laughed as though she'd really burned him on that one. "I guess I didn't blame you—in fact, frankly, I was relieved.

"But then I started getting a different impression in the next couple of days. Lots of . . . mixed messages." He was sparing nothing.

"When I saw the light on in your office today, I decided to stop playing cat-and-mouse games, and just ask you to come hear me out."

Suddenly there was a slight break in Stephen's absolute confidence, but his voice was filled with honesty and integrity. "I guess I'd like to ask at this point . . . how you've been feeling."

Anne closed her eyes as all the defenses she'd worked so hard to maintain fell off her shoulders like heavy weights. She sat there for some time, and when she opened her eyes again, she looked into Stephen's with the same honesty he'd shown her. "Exactly the same." The words came out as a whisper.

Stephen searched her face, only to find the mask pulled down. Then he shook his head slowly and simply lifted his hand and held it out to her. Words had served their purpose.

The next thing she knew, Stephen was gathering her to him like a long-lost child. His kiss was soft and sweet. Delicate and loving. It said everything her heart had longed to hear. Everything she herself felt.

After a long moment he pulled away slightly, his eyes filled with emotion. "Turn around," he said with a hoarse voice.

Of one mind with him, Anne curled her legs against the back of her seat and draped herself across his lap. There was nothing between them now.

For a second their eyes met in silent communication. They were both playing with fire, yet neither could back away.

Stephen drew her slowly to him, but this time his kiss was not soft or reverent. It was full and solid and alive with hunger, almost savage in its possession of her. This was the Stephen she'd longed to meet. The Stephen he'd held back.

All the innate power that she had sensed was hidden seemed to emanate from him now. It seemed to permeate through his body to hers, filling her senses with its magnificent, protective warmth.

Without a thought Anne wrapped her arms around his neck, returning his starred kiss with every ounce of giving she had. Everything between the last time she'd been in his arms and this moment seemed to melt into a fading dream, and she heard her own whimper as she parted her lips under his. She had known it before, and she knew it now. She wanted this man forever.

In a moment of greeting on a new dimension, Anne felt a steady force begin to well up in Stephen's body. It was like a tidal wave out at sea, gathering momentum. She pressed her body more tightly against his, her kiss becoming more intimate. More urgent.

But in the next second she was aware of strong hands on her arms, and breaking away from her lips, Stephen began covering her face with wonderfully forceful little kisses, as though he could never get enough of her. The electric energy that had filled the air would have exploded if left unharnessed, Anne realized; it was his only way of drawing to a close an embrace that wouldn't have found an end in itself.

But his kisses came with such fervor—on her cheeks, her eyelids, her temple, her forehead.

Feeling just as hopelessly wired by a tension that had to be released somewhere, Anne suddenly found Stephen's rush of zealous little kisses desperately funny. Her amused smile must have set him off with the same thought, because the kisses suddenly came faster, each with more zest than the last, until Anne couldn't suppress the laugh rising in her throat. "Stop!"

She had barely been able to get the word out, because as soon as he heard the laugh, Stephen moaned like a delighted caveman between wet smacks. "Mmm. Now this me like! Me want more!"

Anne's laugh turned into an uncontrollable giggle. Was this the man she'd thought of as elegant?

But after a moment the kisses gradually died down, and her laughter along with it, until Stephen finally gathered her up in a bear hug. "God," he sighed. "I just can't make myself leave this woman alone!" He said it as if it were a fact that still amazed him but one that he'd learned to accept.

Still holding her in a possessive hug, Stephen smoothed Anne's hair away from her face, his hands wonderfully rough yet gentle. Finally he pressed her head against his chest.

He smells like home should smell, Anne thought, lifting her face slightly to look at him.

His eyes were closed. He looked so contented just sitting there, enjoying the way she fitted so perfectly into the crook of his arm.

After a long moment Stephen spoke, and Anne felt the vibration of his words through his chest. "Now I don't know whether to be relieved or terrified." He sighed. "It would have been so much easier if you'd just told me to get lost."

"Ah, but I didn't, and I won't. And don't feel alone," she assured him, "because I don't know whether to be relieved or terrified, either—especially after that display you just gave me." Anne heard her familiar soft, lusty laugh. "Mmm, me like," she imitated, burying her nose in his chest. She wanted to keep reality away a little longer.

Stephen left a moment of silence as he thought. "You know, we're going to have to discuss 'the circumstances.'" They had both begun to pronounce it with a pause designed to give the words special meaning.

"Why? We both know that they are—we'll just have to be very discreet, that's all. For the time being, can't we just play it by ear and see what happens?"

"There's a point." Stephen pondered. "In a month we may hate each other, and it'll all be solved by itself." He laughed.

"Don't count on my end of that," said Anne.

"Well, then, I guess the worst that can happen is that we act like thieves in the night for five months—plus a respectable two weeks thrown in just for appearances, of course. Then we come out of hiding looking white as snow." He paused. "No, I suppose it could be even worse than that. I mean, think of the pickle this would be if you were permanent."

Anne felt herself freeze. Stephen knew nothing about the possibility that Trudy wouldn't return, let alone the fact that Anne had bet all her chips on Trudy's *not* returning. Shouldn't she tell him that in five months she planned to be cemented in his firm rather than leaving it?

"On the other hand," he continued, "I guess maybe that's not the worst that could happen, after all. You could hate me in two weeks, and I could still be feeling like I do at this moment—bought and paid for."

Anne relaxed again, putting a hold on her fears. There was no way to predict the future, so why worry about it prematurely? Who knew where anyone would be five months from then? Besides, at this point she couldn't betray Trudy's plans, even if she wanted to. Pushing worries aside, Anne closed her eyes and snuggled closer.

Still stroking the hair away from her face, Stephen sighed once more. "I have to admit I'm pretty uncomfortable with secrecy. But under these circumstances, until things change, I guess that's the only way we can handle . . . those circumstances." Suddenly he burrowed his nose into her hair and scratched his head. "Did that make any sense? At all?" He laughed.

Anne thought for a moment. "Actually, Stephen, under the circumstances it made perfect sense."

"You're disgusting," he accused, shaking his head.

A moment of silence passed with each thinking private thoughts, neither in a hurry to end the silence and neither knowing how to.

Finally Stephen spoke, his voice quiet, almost wistful. "I'll tell you one thing. I've sure never had anyone affect me like this before. I really don't know quite what to do with you."

Anne snuggled against his chest. "Yes, well, God help me when you figure it out," she laughed.

"You know, I was prepared for you to tell me you thought I was insane."

"Well, I suspect you are." Anne pondered her own feelings during the past week. "But then, clearly, so am I." She raised her face enough to look up into his eyes, and melted under the warmth she saw in them.

"Good!" he concluded happily. He said it as though he found insanity a very acceptable condition.

Anne laughed silently, and still entranced by the natural scent she'd already grown to love, she again closed her eyes and buried her face against Stephen's chest. They remained like that, curled up together as they listened to the sound of waves crashing gently below them.

After a while Stephen's gentle stroking on her hair stopped. "Hmm. I just had a thought." He pulled away enough to look into her eyes. "This may seem unceremonious, but do you feel up to driving to Pismo Beach for clams?"

"Food? After this? You must be kidding."

But after dropping an abrupt little kiss on the tip of Stephen's nose, Anne swung herself back into a sitting position. "So? What are you waiting for? I'm ravenous! Drive!"

She quickly retrieved her purse from the floor and pulled out her brush and lipstick. Then she flipped down the sun visor as if this were her car and she'd done so a thousand times before.

After a moment she noticed the way Stephen was looking at her, and she suspended her brush in midair. "Key. Accelerator," she reminded him.

Stephen watched in amazement as she began whipping the brush through her hair, just certain he'd start the car at any moment. After all, Pismo clams didn't sound all that unceremonious.

Finally he shook his head. "Oh, God," he groaned, "what have I let myself in for?" Then with the resigned deliberation of the beaten, he reached for the key.

THE EVENING THEY SPENT TOGETHER was perfect. They sat across from each other, unaware that there was anyone else around. They told each other about their pasts as though they were long-lost friends catching up on years of separation.

Stephen related the happy ending to his ex-wife's crisis. Cathy had decided to move back to Boston and open a ballet school for children. That sounded like a wonderful fairy tale to Anne, but there was the same odd aura of guilt about him that she'd sensed before. She decided not to question it.

It was late when they began the drive back to town, and Anne snuggled against him as they made their way down Pacific Coast Highway toward Santa Monica. But when they entered the little beach community, she knew instinctively that he'd feel more comfortable if she moved farther away. She slid to her side of the seat.

Rounding the corner onto Wilshire Boulevard, Stephen caught sight of a taxi. He honked, motioning the driver alongside the car. Stephen asked him to park and wait for them, handing some money through the windows.

After pulling the Lincoln to the side of the street, Stephen glanced at Anne. There was a slight look of disgust in his eyes as he motioned to the taxi.

"See? This is the part I don't like." The entire area from Santa Monica to Beverly Hills was like a small town, and it seemed disproportionately populated with lawyers. They all knew each other and each other's partners.

Stephen reached across and opened her door. He took her hand and squeezed it. "I have a partners' meeting tomorrow night, but I'll call you during the day."

Suddenly Anne had the irresistible urge to hug him, but she knew she couldn't. He was untouchable again.

5

ANNE HUMMED A SOFT MELODY as she rode up the elevator. Somehow the lights behind the numbers didn't seem to be lighting anymore. Now they were twinkling. Everything looked different.

She had driven home in an almost dreamlike state, playing back in her mind the afternoon and evening, reliving, over and over again, the feel of Stephen's arms around her. She couldn't stop thinking about what it would be like to have him make love to her.

So where's your conservative approach now, dummy? Anne kept giving herself affectionate warnings, having always believed that lovemaking was something very special, to be strictly reserved for a time when a relationship had worked through all other aspects.

Yet this man...her feelings about him were deeper than any she'd ever had before, and she wasn't used to having to pull any reins on her emotions. It felt strange to find herself doing it now. But then nothing else was typical about Stephen, so why should her feelings about him follow any set pattern, either?

"Love" Stephen? Maybe not. But "in love" with Stephen? Definitely. Most definitely.

Turning where the large original oil hung on the wall, separating the two sides of the suite, Anne sang her way to her office. As she rounded the corner into her private domain, she immediately noticed the note on her desk. Mr. Tomlin wanted to see her as soon as she arrived.

Just as she was reading it, her phone rang. Then no sooner did she hang up from the dictating machine vendor when her other line rang. Yes, things were feeling normal!

"Anne Michaels," she answered, her voice ringing happily.

"Hi." It was Stephen.

"Oh, it's you," she said, exaggerating a bored, dreary voice.

There was a long pause. "Well, I guess I have the wrong number," he said stiffly. Then he hung up.

Anne stood there with her mouth open. *Oh, my God, he took me seriously!* She had started to dial his number when her other line rang. *Get rid of them,* she thought, impatiently punching the other button.

"Hi." It was Stephen again, his voice exactly the same.

Anne grinned. "What in the world are you doing?"

"Playing stupid games with your brain." He laughed. "Want to go sailing tomorrow night after work?" His voice was enticing.

"Tomorrow . . . night?"

"Mmm! It's a great place to sneak away with your favorite clandestine friend."

"I've never been sailing before."

"Poor, sheltered girl. Listen, you'll love this little sweetheart. She's a thirty-eight foot trimaran. She sails flat, so you can't get seasick. A friend of mine owns her, and he and his girlfriend are going to take her out to test some new radio equipment he bought. They invited me—us—to go along."

"It's not an attorney, is it?"

"Uh, yeah. Damn! How did you know? In fact, it's Cooper's son."

Anne gasped.

"Of course it's not an attorney!" Stephen laughed at her gullibility. "It's one of my other friends—he's a psychiatrist.

Well, actually, he's better described as a sailor who practices psychiatry when he's weathered in. But you'll like him. He'll probably turn your head, in fact."

Anne smiled to herself. "My head doesn't turn very easily. Especially with you in my line of vision."

"That's good. I'd hate to have to throw a good shrink overboard."

Anne pictured a younger version of Tomlin. "How big is he?"

"Six-three." Anne could hear Stephen's other line ring. "Hold on a minute." He put her on hold and then came back sounding official. "It's Philadelphia—talk to you later." He clicked off.

After several minutes had passed, Anne realized that she'd been sitting there in the same position, her hand still on the instrument. A silly smile had come to her face—she'd almost been flirting with the doorknob that happened to be in her line of vision.

Suddenly she laughed, shaking her head. How embarrassing it would have been if someone had popped his head in just then. "There's Anne," he'd say, "grinning at the doorknob like a feebleminded lunatic."

She sat back, breaking the spell with a long stretch. But upon the final, satisfied groan, her eyes fell to Tomlin's note, and the words "as soon as possible." She snapped back to reality.

Quickly stuffing her purse into a bottom drawer, Anne rushed to Tomlin's office. On the way she heard a mournful "Oh, no!" then a lawyer's door closing ever so quietly.

Tomlin motioned for her to come in. He was just finishing scratching his tiny, precise signature on a stack of correspondence. Then, setting it aside with a deliberate motion, he peered tiredly across the desk to where Anne had taken a seat.

She couldn't read the expression on his face, but it was something like grave boredom.

"Mr. Butler has had a little accident," he patiently began. "I would like you to send him a large, flamboyant flower arrangement from the firm. He's at Cedars Sinai Hospital."

"Oh, dear!" Anne exclaimed. "Is it serious?"

Tomlin looked at her plaintively, laying his pen on the desk as he sighed. "It seems the walnut tree in front of young Butler's house needed trimming. The fellow he'd retained didn't show up as planned yesterday, so Timothy fancied he'd do the surgery himself."

Tomlin's tone was measured, and he cleared his throat before continuing. "It seems he became so involved with his artistic endeavors that he zestfully cut off the branch...upon which he was sitting."

"What?" The word came out as a slow whisper as Anne sank back in her chair.

Mr. Tomlin smiled understandingly. "Mr. Butler gets extremely, shall we say, 'carried away' with a project."

"My Lord!" She was too shocked to acknowledge the pun. "How far did he fall?"

"Twenty feet." He enunciated the words.

"Twenty feet!" she gasped. "How badly hurt was he?"

"He broke a leg, cracked two ribs and sprained his elbow. A few cuts and bruises beyond that."

"Oh, Mr. Tomlin!" Anne's bracelets clinked together as she slowly placed four fingers over her mouth. "Oh, the—the poor fellow!" *Don't, Anne,* she cautioned herself. *Whatever you do, don't!*

Just when she thought she had herself under control, Anne felt her face suddenly contort, and then she heard her own peal of hysterical laughter.

There was deadly silence from Tomlin's side of the desk and as soon as she could catch her breath, Anne forced herself into grave soberness. "I know I shouldn't find this funny, Mr. Tomlin—"

But it was no use. In the next second she was doubled over in her chair, covering her face with her hands, all hope now dashed.

Tomlin sat there biting his lip and looking out the window. "You have a perfectly wretched sense of humor, my dear." He waited for her to stop.

After a long moment of praying for control, Anne heard Tomlin's voice become a quaver of failing self-restraint. "I can just see him—" he finally rasped.

Then, without warning, Tomlin flung his thin hands in the air to make an imaginary camera, his eyes squinting with a faraway look. "There sits Timothy, and the scene begins! Intense, glazed eyes! The sweat absolutely *beading* on a furtive brow as he works with unyielding, dedicated purpose!

"We watch his face mirror a steel-trap mind as he diligently saws. And the branch gets thinner...and thinner...." Tomlin's eyes were now gleaming wildly.

"Stop!" Anne begged, making a weak plea.

Tomlin's frail body began shaking, and finally he pulled out his handkerchief and dabbed at streaming eyes, handing Anne a tissue from his side drawer as a considerate afterthought.

As soon as they had recovered, Anne returned to her office to check her mascara before anyone saw her. Not everyone would be as understanding as Tomlin.

He was really beginning to surprise her. She would have expected him to just sit there, horrified at her reaction. But the way he'd pronounced her sense of humor, "perfectly wretched, my dear" said something about his own.

By ten o'clock the whole firm was buzzing, disbelieving gasps audible in every corner. Poor Timothy Butler, thought Anne. He was an outstanding lawyer, so single-minded and meticulous that not even the tiniest detail escaped his scrutiny. But Butler sometimes missed the obvious, Anne had been warned. It was just a trait of his, and everyone worked around it.

After calling the florist, Anne spent the rest of the day negotiating final quotes with the dictating machine reps. She was interrupted occasionally for other things, and by late afternoon she came to a stopping point. All reports had been directed to the appropriate people, and nothing further could be started without hearing the outcome of the partners' meeting.

Waiting only long enough to see that the meeting had got under way, Anne left for the day. She'd pack a choice of sailing clothes to accommodate any weather condition. Then she'd take a long, hot bath and make it an early evening.

THE NEXT MORNING Anne waited at her desk, hoping for an early call from Tomlin. But once again he called at exactly nine-thirty.

As she took the chair across from him, he began telling her some of the things that had been discussed in the partners' meeting. She was to order the dictating machines she'd recommended, and he added that the partners were quite pleased with the terms. So far, so good.

"What about the policy and benefit report?"

Tomlin arched an eyebrow. "Well, your report was rather . . . vague, shall we say. It basically said that as far as you could tell, we need to investigate tighter structure along with more defined benefits and policies."

"But that's true."

Mr. Tomlin blinked his eyes several times. "But we know that. I believe that was the assignment itself, was it not?"

Oops, thought Anne. She should have dispensed with the single sheet of generalities and just waited until she had something concrete to say. But she'd given in to her eagerness to demonstrate that the review was under way, and that was a sure sign of an amateur. "I guess I'll need more time to give you anything specific," she said, suddenly feeling foolish.

Tomlin's smile was fatherly. "That's all right, my dear. Zestfulness eventually gets replaced by wisdom. Enjoy it while you can." At least he was trying to be helpful.

Then the smile turned into a laugh. "Besides, what's thirty seconds of eleven busy partners' time in order for each of them to jointly and severally determine the page they're all reading says absolutely nothing? Pshaw, we do it all the time," he concluded, waving his hand.

They just can't resist. Even the best of them, Anne thought. "I'll refrain in the future," she offered, clearing her throat.

At an appropriate time Anne asked how Butler was doing.

Tomlin laughed sardonically. "He'll survive, I'm afraid. Oh, that reminds me. . . ."

He began jotting a note to himself, and Anne waited as he kept writing and writing, mumbling to himself and glancing at his watch. She began to wonder if he'd forgotten she was there.

He was such a twinkling old soul. Having got to know him a bit, Anne was discovering that all the quirks she'd heard about were just part of his personality, and amazingly harmless.

"Incidentally. . ." he continued vaguely as he finished his note. "Merrifield's going to take Butler's place in New York and Washington, and he tends to procrastinate. I want to send an interim billing that will cover his Philadelphia trip, so get an accurate accounting of his expenses before letting him get on another plane, would you?"

Anne didn't flicker an eyelash. "Sure. How long will he be gone?"

"Well, Butler's work in D.C. would take hopefully no longer than a week, but he was going to handle a matter for me in New York first. That'll take two weeks. Then Merrifield has another week in Philadelphia, so it'll be about a month in all."

Anne winced inside. *A month?*

Tomlin smiled. "You don't know Merrifield yet, but if you let him leave without getting his paperwork, we'll never see it."

"How long do I—" She quickly rephrased the question. "When is he leaving?"

"Tomorrow late afternoon. Make sure Eileen doesn't have any trouble booking him, would you?"

"Okay," she agreed, relieved that Tomlin was wrapping up the discussion.

Once she was back in her office, she dialed Stephen's extension. *"Damn!"* she said as she waited for an answer. "Hi, Eileen. Is Merrifield in?"

"No, he's at the hospital with Mr. Butler, but I just talked to him, and they were almost finished. Poor man, he was so happy to get back, and now he's off again."

Don't rub it in. "Yes, well, I'm going to need his Philadelphia expenses before he goes. He hasn't given them to you by any chance, has he?"

"Only a few receipts. My dear, you're in for a battle," Eileen warned, her tone one of motherly tolerance. "He procrastinates on those—and time sheets. It's like prying a bone away from a dog."

"Yes, I've heard," Anne said. "Is there anything you can put together to start it off? I promised Mr. Tomlin I'd get it right away. He wants to bill it out."

"Well, I'll just type up what I have right now, and Stephen can fill in the blanks. Darn," Eileen added. "With Stephen having just been gone for a month, I'm all caught up on everything. The very idea of another month without him here just fills me with dread."

"Believe me, Eileen, I can certainly understand that." Anne grimaced. "Have you booked his reservations?"

"Oh, yes, he's all set. His tickets will be delivered this afternoon or the first thing tomorrow morning. They'll come to you for approval, so if they're not here by nine-thirty, could you let me know?"

"Sure. I'm glad you told me." They hung up. "Damn, damn, damn the luck!" Anne slammed her drawer shut so hard that all the pencils crashed against the back panel.

As soon as Stephen returned, he called. She closed her door.

"Well, it looks like I'm off again." He sounded disgusted.

"So I heard. *Yuk!* And of course since you have to leave tomorrow afternoon, I suppose that cancels tonight."

"The hell it does," he said softly.

Anne's heart leaped as she felt a smile forming. "It's still on?"

"I don't see why not. I don't have much to do at home before leaving—just stop at the cleaner's, which I can do on my way in tomorrow morning. It won't take me any time to pack, since by now I've memorized every article."

"Wonderful," Anne breathed. At least they'd have one evening. Then her glance fell to her book. "Oh! I almost forgot! Listen, Stephen, I told Mr. Tomlin I'd get your expenses before letting you get on another plane."

"Oh, yes. Well, I can send them to you from—"

"No." She cut him off. "Please—he wants to bill out the client, and I promised I'd get them from you before you left."

She could hear the avoidance. "Anne, you just have no idea how busy—"

"Please? Pretty please?"

There was a long pause. "All right," he grumbled finally. "It shouldn't take that long, I guess."

"I've been warned what a procrastinator you are on administrative details, so do them now," she coaxed.

"Listen, let me talk to you about it tonight. I've got some things I need to get out."

"Yes, you do. Start with your expense account."

"Good God, woman!" Stephen roared. "What have I gotten myself into?" But then his voice lowered to a whisper. "Only for you would I do this."

As soon as they hung up, Anne called Tomlin to tell him she'd secured Stephen's solemn promise.

"Good girl!" he said heartily.

She hesitated a moment. "Mr. Tomlin, I was hoping to leave a little early this afternoon. Would it be possible for me to skip out around four?"

"Of course! Leave whenever you need to."

"Thank you. I'll get Merrifield's expenses to you as soon as they're typed."

"Good! I like to have things in hand."

"I know," she said, laughing. That was his favorite phrase.

Anne dropped by Stephen's office around two-thirty, and he was on the phone. He motioned her in and handed her his expenses, all typed and ready to get fed into the computer.

Anne made a big show of being impressed, and as Stephen listened to the party on the other end of the phone, he pulled a sheet of paper from his desk drawer. "Directions to the boat," he silently mouthed.

Anne looked them over to be sure she understood them. They were amazingly detailed. "What time?" she whispered.

He covered the mouthpiece. "As early as you can get there."

"I'm leaving at four."

"Grreeeat!" he whispered, winking. In the same stroke he returned to his conversation. "Excuse me, Howard. You've asked for four extensions, which I've accommodated, because you weren't even prepared. Don't start haggling with me on a flimsy point like that...."

6

MARINA DEL REY WAS only twenty minutes from the office, but once inside the little boating community, Anne felt as if she'd entered another world.

That was her favorite thing about the Los Angeles area. It was so diverse. Beverly Hills was a world unto itself. The beach communities, each slightly different, were another; the canyons, yet another. And one hadn't even scratched the surface of anything east of the famous Rodeo Drive.

As Anne's little white car slowly made its way down Admiralty Way past the gardened condominiums and high-rent apartments, she scanned the numerous side streets. On each of them she could see solid lines of more condominiums.

Knowing that the boat slips were behind them, Anne pondered how marvelous it must be to step out on your balcony for morning coffee and look out onto a vast array of yachts.

There it was. Panay Way, well announced by a big sign. Now all she had to do was find the parking structure Stephen had marked. One look at the massive complex told her why he'd drawn such a meticulous map.

Following his written directions, Anne pulled up to the box and dialed the number as instructed. A voice answered, and Anne read the code number. After a second the gate lifted by remote control. "There you go," said the voice.

Once on the other side, Anne entered the structure, and passing Stephen's car, she drove up to the second level to leave hers. After all, who knew what local lawyer might be living in one of those units. Unaccustomed as she was to sneaking around, she was half enjoying it. It was like playing detective.

Finally outside on the walkway leading to the docks, Anne stopped for just a moment. The steady tinkling of lines against metal masts sounded like music from a fairyland orchestra, and the smell of the sea filled the air with its pungent crispness.

Anne's eyes swept over the landscape of boats in front of her. The hulls and tarps formed an irregular checkerboard pattern of blue, gold and white. Not one vessel looked incapable of making a sea crossing. For a moment Anne wondered if she should have spent her lunch hour shopping for a white duck sailing outfit, something casually respectful of yachting tradition.

She began walking as her eyes scanned each slip gate for the letter *C*. Stephen's instructions had even included how to get through the gate if it was locked, but she was relieved to see it had been left ajar.

Even if Anne hadn't known the boat's exact location, she'd have noticed it. Sitting on three rocketlike hulls, the trimaran spread itself out like an octopus on the water. As she walked the length of it toward the stern, she heard music coming from inside. There was no one on deck.

Hesitating briefly, Anne then knocked softly on the side of the boat. She wouldn't have been at all surprised if someone had emerged in a blue captain's hat with a gold-twined anchor on the front, yelling "Ahoy!"

Instead a woman with long, naturally-curly blond hair and no makeup popped her head out of the cabin.

"Hi!" she called, swinging herself onto the deck. She was wearing faded cutoff jeans and a sweatshirt that looked six sizes too big, and her tanned legs looked trim and muscular as she climbed barefoot over the cockpit toward Anne.

"So much for worrying about yacht club dress codes," said Anne.

"Amen," she said with a laugh. "You must be Anne." Kneeling, she reached for the duffel bag and tossed it onto the seat in the cockpit.

"I'm Terri," she said, smiling. "Hand me your shoes so you won't slip." It was a tactful way of protecting the deck.

Slipping them off, Anne watched slender hands pull at the dock tie. It seemed as if it would be a futile effort, but the huge white hulk obediently lazed its way closer to the dock steps.

"I'm amazed," said Anne, preparing to climb aboard.

"Don't be—it's just a big puppy dog. Wait just a sec," Terri said, pressing down a rope that would have been an unpleasant obstacle for Anne in her suit. "Here, take my hand. The boat rocks slightly when you climb aboard."

After making her unsteady way onto the deck, Anne followed Terri over the hull to the cockpit. It seemed so strange to be crawling across a boat in a business suit.

"Stephen and Wil went to the market to pick up some snacks, but they should be back any minute. Would you like to change? Want a Coke?" Terri just seemed to bubble it all out at once.

Anne laughed, liking her immediately. "Yes, and yes," she replied. Picking up her bag, she followed the leader into the cabin.

Terri motioned over her shoulder. "You can try to change in the head if you want, but it's easier right here. I'll stand guard in case they come back," she offered, peeping out the cabin top. She began chipping ice off a small block.

"This is quite some boat," Anne said, slipping out of her suit skirt.

"Oh, I just love multihulls. They don't list, so you're not always walking on the walls. And you don't get seasick!"

Anne raised her eyebrows in appreciation. "Well, this is my first time on a boat, so I'm glad to hear that. Are they safe?" She laughed a little nervously.

"Oh, sure! I've heard of them getting into trouble in really high winds with someone who doesn't know what they're doing, but both Wil and I are fair weather sailors."

Anne zipped up her jeans. "Stephen said Wil really sails a lot."

"Ah, but we have a lot of fair weather." Terri's laugh came readily.

Tugging the short sleeved cotton pullover out of her bag, Anne put it on before taking a sip from the wide-bottomed plastic mug Terri had set down in front of her.

"So you're the lady who's turned Stepehn's head." Terri grinned as she dried the last of some dishes. Her tone was sisterly.

Anne shrugged, blushing slightly. "Do you know Stephen well?"

"Oh, I've known him forever. Wil's a client of Stephen's old firm. His sense of humor is possibly even a little sicker than Stephen's, so they became good friends right away."

Anne rolled her eyes and laughed understandingly. "Then I can't imagine either of them in anything other than law or medicine. Can I help you?"

"No. Just sit and relax. I'm just straightening up the galley for the sail." She was securing everything as if preparing for an earthquake, and Anne cringed.

"So you're temporarily running Stephen's law firm?"

"Well, I wouldn't call it 'running' the firm. I'm filling in for their office manager who's out with back surgery."

"That's what Stephen said. I was amazed he was actually dating someone in his own firm, but he said it was temporary. She'll be back in what, five months?"

Anne's stomach churned slightly. "That's the plan, poor thing. She really had a lot of pain, sitting and standing all day." As soon as it was a natural time to change the subject, she did. "Do you work?"

"Yes. But in my job it's feast or famine. I work for a film writer, and we get paid by the script. So when we're working I get called in day, night and weekends. Then when it's over, I'm free till another one."

Anne took a sip of her Coke. "That must be nice."

"It's great when we're not working but really hectic otherwise. We just finished a biggie, so I'm unemployed for a while. I'm so glad," she continued as she wiped down the sink. "It's great to have a summer free."

Anne heard a loud thud from the side of the boat.

"Oh! Here they are," said Terri, popping her head out as she had before. Anne's heart did a light, quick leap in her chest.

"Hello, in there!" It was Stephen's resonant voice. The boat rocked as he climbed aboard, his footsteps echoing into the cabin. Then it rocked again.

Stephen came down the stairs and greeted Anne with an approving smile. "You look cute." Setting the two bags on the table, he kissed her briefly.

"So do you," she teased as her eyes surveyed old white pants and a faded blue workshirt that set off his ruddy complexion. Now she was doubly glad she hadn't thought of the shopping trip—she'd really have been out of place.

Stephen motioned to Wil, and Anne realized she hadn't even acknowledged his presence.

As tall as Stephen but leaner, Wil had twinkling, deep-set eyes that suggested a personality as mischievous as Stephen's. But Anne grinned to see the traditional Freudian beard. It somehow screamed "Psychiatrist!" Nevertheless, it was difficult to imagine anyone taking serious problems to this light-hearted sort.

"Hi!" he chirped. He'd been chewing on a carrot, which he stuck into his pocket, wiping his fingers on his pants before he shook hands with her.

Anne's eyes followed the carrot.

"Oh, that's one thing I forgot to tell you about Wil," said Stephen. "The carrot is his trademark. He's never without one."

Wil continued chomping. "It's my security." He patted his pocket protectively.

As soon as all the groceries were stowed away, everyone went up on deck to help with the ceremony of undocking the boat. Following a tactful suggestion, Anne kept out of the way and watched the other three move in coordinated effort. Once the engine was fired up, Terri untied the dock line, jumping precariously back onto the boat just in time before it moved away from the dock area.

Anne settled back and watched the other boats coming and going. It was all so organized, with each showing courtesy you'd never find on the streets. It wasn't cold, as she'd expected, and she sat in fascination as the sails of the trimaran unfurled. Terri climbed all over the boat like a monkey, unwrapping lines, pulling sleeves off sails and storing little ties into neat bundles here and there.

In no time they were out of the marina and under full sail. Then Stephen shut off the engine. After the momentary shock of sudden silence, Anne noticed the soft rush of water against the hulls.

"Oh, this is magnificent," she said as Stephen stretched out on the seat beside her.

He placed his feet on a hump that doubled as engine cover and coffee table, draping his arm around her shoulders. "It's a tolerable way to spend an evening," he conceded.

Anne laughed. "No kidding. But I thought boats rocked sideways." There was a delightfully gentle to and fro bucking-horse motion.

"Mono-hulls," Stephen reminded her, kissing her on the cheek. The warmth of his lips contrasted with the cool sea breeze, and Anne snuggled against him as she watched Wil at the tiller.

Terri had disappeared into the cabin as soon as the sails had been raised, and Anne was just about to ask about her when she emerged with the most beautiful array of food Anne had ever seen. Crackers and cheese, cold cuts, marinated artichoke hearts, shrimp and fruit, all artfully arranged on a platter.

With everyone raving in anticipation, Wil finished hooking up the automatic steering device while the other three distributed plates, napkins and poured the fine Cabernet into thin acrylic wine goblets made especially for boats.

Anne was glad to see she wasn't the only starving person on board, because ten minutes went by with little conversation. The shrimp sauce had just the right piquancy so as not to conflict with the artichoke hearts, and somehow the two made a graceful companion to the cheese.

Wil was a riot, Anne thought as she crunched into a slice of cold apple. He did keep a carrot in his pocket all the time, and he actually seemed to check on it periodically to be sure it was still there. Maybe he hadn't been joking about it being his security. But she'd never met a normal psychiatrist yet, so she was prepared to accept anything.

After they'd eaten Anne sat back, amazed at the quantity she'd devoured. "I've never been so hungry," she excused herself, laughing.

"Nothing like camping or sailing to make you want to eat like a hog," said Wil. He patted Terri's stomach disdainfully as he gave her a look of reproach. Yet he'd devoured the lion's share, and Terri had eaten less than any of them.

"We humor him," Terri explained.

"Anne, they just think that," said Wil. "It's the only way they can keep their sanity. You know, blaming everything on me."

Terri winked. "As I said, we humor him."

Anne laughed. *The man must be a real challenge to live with on a daily basis. Cute, though.*

Anne and Stephen watched as Wil settled back into the long white-cushioned seat. He'd dug out his new radio equipment, and suddenly oblivious to their presence, he admired it contentedly as he read the specifications.

After a moment Terri joined him, seeming every bit as enthralled. She helped him try to figure out the directions for installing it, and within moments they were lost in a world of wires and connectors and diagrams.

Lying down on the seat, Stephen laid his head in her lap. "Do you mind?" He looked up at her.

"You must be kidding," Anne said, running her fingers through his hair.

He closed his eyes, and she sat back, enjoying the wine as she took in the sight of the shoreline a half mile away. It could have been a million miles away, as far as she was concerned.

Glancing across the boat, Anne noticed the movement of the tiller. She became fascinated by the way the automatic pilot made tiny, efficient corrections to their course. Except for someone's having to stand up every few minutes to look around for other boats or buoys, it was effortless sailing.

That was a relief. For some reason, she'd half expected that everyone would be frantically trying to keep the thing afloat. But this was wonderful. The sound of the water, the wind, the total peace. Anne let her thoughts roam.

"What's funny?" murmured Stephen after a while, his eyes still closed.

"Wil. He looks like a little kid playing with his first erector set."

"Don't tell him that, he'll go on a harangue about Freudian slips."

"Oh, don't tell me he's one of those."

"No, but he loves to pretend he is. I don't know, though, he's awfully convincing."

They lapsed again into comfortable silence, each enjoying the moments that ticked by all too fast.

Suddenly Anne noticed it was getting dark. It seemed as though such a short time had passed and when she commented on the change, Stephen mentioned it more loudly to Wil, since it would take a while to get back.

"Oh, that's the problem!" Wil squinted out to sea. He'd been trying to read the owner's manual, holding it closer and closer in the failing light.

Stephen groaned at the interruption to the peace he'd found. Cradling his head in her lap, Anne had been half hypnotizing him with little drawings on his forehead. But before he got up to take the tiller, she erased them all with a brisk rub.

Anne watched with interest as they prepared to change directions. Terri took the steering device off and turned the boat into the wind. "Coming about," she said. Everyone seemed to be waiting for something to happen, when suddenly Wil gave one hard yank on a huge rope that had been locked into a steel trap.

Then everything seemed to happen at once. Wil's rope began whipping like a crazed snake, disappearing through the crankcase with amazing speed. Stephen had another one just like it on the other side of the cockpit, and he was rapidly reeling the same length into coils.

"Don't ever let a foot get caught in one of these," Wil said, calling Anne's attention to the circles as they got sucked through the crankcase. Anne shuddered at the thought of it, but she saw that he was watching the line carefully to be sure it didn't snag or pigtail.

As soon as the boat had turned fully around, Terri got on the course she wanted and reset the automatic pilot while Stephen fine-tuned the sail.

Wil had already returned to his radio, and within seconds he was sitting there with a flashlight, scratching his head as he pondered the next step. Once again he was lost to the world.

"Well, that was certainly exciting," said Anne as Stephen sat next to her, looping the line into a neat pile.

"It looks more frantic than it is," he explained. "The reason everyone works so fast is that if the boat points in the wrong direction before the wind fills the sail from the other side, it's a real pain in the neck to get it turned around again—it's called 'being in irons.'"

Anne noticed that the wind seemed distinctly calmer since they'd turned around, and she was just about to ask about it when Terri emerged from the galley with a tray to gather their dishes.

"Here, let me help you," Anne said, getting to her feet.

"Not a chance," Terri smiled. "You and Stephen won't see each other for a month, and this won't take but a minute. Besides, it's easier in the galley with just one person." Terri turned to Stephen. "Why don't you show Anne up to the bow and enjoy the moon on the water for a while. That's one of the best parts of sailing, and we can't let her go home without seeing how beautiful it all is."

"That sounds like an excellent idea," agreed Stephen. He reached out to take Anne's hand.

As he guided her carefully toward the front of the boat, Anne sniffed the air. "Why is it so calm?" she asked. "It was so different before we turned around."

"We're going with the wind now—it doesn't even feel much like we're moving, but we are."

Stephen climbed over a rope to sit down against the wall of the cabin, which curved into a ready-made lounge chair. Bracing his feet, he extended a hand to help Anne.

Climbing over his leg, she managed to lower herself into the space he'd left for her to sit in front of him, sled style.

As soon as she'd settled, Stephen reclined against the cabin, pulling her back against his chest as he wrapped his arms around her like a big blanket. There was a slight chill in the air, and the warmth of Stephen's body was welcome.

It took a moment for their eyes to adjust to the light of the moon without the glare from the cabin, but as they did, it was a beautiful sight to behold. The water was dark except for the little flashes of moonlight that danced on the peaks of the waves, and as they sat there, Anne marveled at how well she could see.

"This is the joy of a night sail," said Stephen. Even though the three hulls cutting through the water made a sloshing noise all around them, Stephen's lips were so close that he was able to whisper in her ear and still be heard.

After a moment she turned her head to the side. She could feel the steady beat of his heart, and she closed her eyes to block out everything but Stephen's nearness.

They said nothing for a long time, listening to the water against the boat as they were rocked gently by the motion of the sea.

"I love your arms around me," Anne said, wishing she could preserve the moment forever.

Stephen lowered his head next to hers as if sensing she'd said something.

She lifted her head so she could speak into his ear, but it was too hard to talk that way. With glances they agreed not to try. Anne settled back against his chest, and her eyes surveyed the width of the boat, noticing all the little places one could lie down. Knowing Stephen couldn't hear her, she mused, "I wonder what it would be like to make love out here."

"Fantastic," he whispered directly into her ear. She could feel him grin from ear to ear.

Anne jumped and swung her head around.

Stephen met her eyes with feigned innocence, holding out his hands in a helpless gesture. "I had my ear against the side of your head." He started to laugh at the shock on her face. "Close your mouth," he added.

She tried to suppress the smile she felt creeping over her face. "You rat." Haughtily turning her back on him once more, she plunked herself hard against his chest.

The soft laugh in her ear gave her goose bumps. "Ah, you're delightful," he said, affectionately hugging her closer. After a moment he turned her into a sideways position for a kiss.

Anne moved her head in teasing defiance as she curled up her legs. "Oh, no, you don't. Not after a trick like that."

Stephen lifted her away from him so she could see the determination on his face. "Oh, yes, I do," he said. His eyes twinkled in the darkness.

Pulling her close, Stephen met no resistance as he covered her mouth with his. The wind blew through her hair, sending a cool breeze to caress her, the warmth of his embrace even more protective by contrast. Anne returned his kiss tentatively at first, but she felt her whole body weaken under the warmth of his lips.

The pressure of Stephen's kiss lightened for just a second before he took her chin in his hand and lost himself in the softness of her mouth. Anne felt his tongue slide slowly across her lips, and she parted them in acceptance, feeling every fiber in her body come alive.

Stephen hesitated again and then, answering the momentum of his own need for her, he crushed her hungrily to him, his kiss becoming more urgent.

While Anne found herself responding more forcefully, she was vaguely aware of Stephen's movements as he slid her arm around his neck so he could free his hands, which dived into her hair, destroying any semblance of order that the sea winds had left.

Just when she thought she'd experienced the ultimate intensity a kiss could possibly reach, Anne felt her own breathing change, and when she heard what sounded like a whimper, she realized it had come from her. Suddenly every organ in her body seemed to melt all at once.

Beyond thinking, she rolled over, guided by an urge to stretch her torso to fill the length of his. She pressed every part of her body tightly against him, lost in the abandon of her very soul, which begged to be joined with his.

Stephen's breathing quickened, which drove her on and on to create a torment that would make him journey with her toward the essence of nature itself.

But then Stephen seemed to be struggling with himself, caught between not wanting to let her go and knowing he must. Anne was too entranced by the power of sensation to help him make any decisions.

With a low, tortured moan, Stephen finally tore himself away from their kiss, his eyes searching Anne's for one intense second. Every muscle in his body had become taut, and without his realizing it, his fingers had dug almost painfully into her arms.

"Good God," he moaned, tilting his head back as he covered his face with his hands. Finally he parted his fingers and peered at her unbelievingly from between them.

Anne felt every bit as shaken as he, and realizing how far she'd let herself go, she reached out and touched his arm. "Stephen, are you okay?"

He looked at her as though she'd gone mad. "Am I . . . okay?" With no warning whatsoever, he slowly raised his fists to the sky as a groan began from behind clenched teeth and mounted to the most animalistic roar Anne had ever heard.

"Stephen!" Anne gasped. She stared at him in shocked fascination. The man had absolutely no inhibitions!

But the next moment was filled with the sound of running footsteps, and Anne clapped her hand over her mouth, suddenly realizing that Stephen's scream had reverberated through the night air. Within seconds Wil was there, panic-stricken. He'd shot out of the cabin like a light.

When he saw them both sitting there, he just stared at them; he was panting and totally disoriented. Then his eyes dropped to the lifesaving ring in his hand. He seemed to be wondering where he'd gotten it. "What the hell happened?" he croaked.

Stephen just looked at him weakly as if every ounce of strength had been sapped from him. "She kissed me," he said simply.

Wil's eyes darted to Anne's as though Stephen's explanation couldn't possibly be taken seriously. But when all he got was a shrug, his face slowly relaxed. Slumping across the top of the cabin, he swallowed hard. "For God's sake, Merrifield, I thought someone had fallen overboard!"

Anne and Stephen just looked at each other and then back at him, guilt shadowing both their faces.

Watching them, Wil slowly shook his head in disgust. He looked at the ring once more as though it irritated him. Then he turned back toward the cabin and, making his way carefully, disappeared.

After he'd gone Stephen just stared at Anne for a moment before dropping an arm onto his knee. "Now what's so damned funny?" he demanded, seeming amazed to find her clutching her sides, laughing hysterically.

After a respectable wait, they returned to the cabin to see if Wil was really angry. Anne was fascinated to note several closely gnawed carrot ends on the seat next to him. "Really got me there, old buddy," said Wil. "I can't say sailing with you is dull."

Anne noticed the look on Terri's face. She'd been staring at Stephen with a grin, and then her eyes met Anne's. "If you guys should ever get married, I'd sure like to hear about your wedding night from whoever has the room next to yours," she said, shaking her head.

By the time they neared the marina, Wil had almost completed hooking up the final connection, so Stephen and Terri shared the task of starting the engine and collapsing the sails. There were almost no other boats out by this time, and a layer of fog was beginning to roll in.

Anne had offered to help with whatever she could, but there was nothing. She sat quietly out of the way to watch, sipping the cup of hot tea Terri had made. It had been such a perfect way to spend the evening. If only it didn't have to end so soon.

After saying good-night Anne and Stephen began the walk back to the parking area, past lights that shone behind the curtains of the liveaboard boats. There was a layer of moisture on the metal ramp, and the sky suddenly seemed black.

Once again Anne listened to the sound of the shrouds hitting the masts. The chorus of tinkling bells seemed to be saying goodbye, growing fainter with every step they took toward the parking garage.

A car entered, its wheels squealing shrilly from quickly rounded turns as it climbed to an upper floor. It was a rude final awakening. They were now back in the world.

Suddenly Anne felt a sadness overtake her as the thought of Stephen's month-long absence hit her full force. "Oh, Stephen." She sighed grimly. "I wish you didn't have to go."

"I know." His voice was soft and pensive. "I'll call you, though." It was a weak consolation for them both.

"Are you coming into the office tomorrow?"

"For a few hours. I'm going to have Greg drive me to the airport."

As they trudged up the stairs Anne thought of the first day she'd met Stephen. "Greg worships you, judging from the look on his face that day when he was in your office."

"That's not worship," Stephen corrected modestly. "Young associates grab every chance they can to discuss the way a case is going. He's run up against a tough opposing attorney in a matter he's just inherited, and after getting slaughtered in several telephone conversations, Greg finally got a lick in. He couldn't wait to tell somebody about it."

"And K&W's litigation 'red hot' is just 'somebody'?"

Stephen laughed as he tossed Anne's bag into the back seat. He leaned on the car, pulling her close against him. "I wish I could take you with me," he murmured, nuzzling his face into her hair.

After a moment he tilted Anne's chin up. "I'm going to miss you," he whispered, kissing her softly. There was a sweet sadness in his eyes.

On impulse, Anne threw her arms around his neck and hugged him tightly. She wanted to memorize every message her senses could pick up. She buried her face in his chest as though to hide from the coming goodbye.

After a long moment Stephen gave her a measured squeeze. "Let's get you in the car. This isn't going to get any easier."

Nodding assent, Anne grudgingly climbed into the driver's seat and started the engine, hating the fact that it turned over. Stephen kissed her once more through the window, each of them lingering long enough to imprint a memory that would have to carry them through the coming thirty days.

At last Stephen brushed her cheek briefly with his hand. "A month," he whispered. Then he walked away.

For a moment Anne tried to persuade herself that Stephen's absence might be a blessing in disguise. That it would give her time to sort things out and get him in perspective. But in the next instant she remained stubbornly unconvinced.

7

ANNE SPENT THE FOLLOWING DAYS calling firms roughly the size of Kimble & Watson to see what she could find out about their policy and benefit packages. First she singled out the managers with the best reputations. *Might as well kill two birds with one stone and get to know the competition.*

As long phone conversations and luncheons brought out the answers she was after, Anne began developing an overall picture of what she was starting and where she wanted to go—not only in terms of K&W's policies, but also her own career.

Basing her conclusions on the people she'd met, she realized that one thing had become obvious. This was a sink or swim proposition she'd gotten herself into by taking over for Trudy, because the competition was stiff.

The more involved Anne became with work, the more she waited for some of the frightening intensity of her feelings for Stephen to dissipate. But her hopes were in vain. In spite of the activity, she thought of him every other minute, got twinges whenever she walked by his office. And her heart leaped whenever the phone rang at home.

Stephen himself contributed little to being forgotten. Their evening conversations were long and unhurried, with him refusing to be reminded of the cost. Instead he argued that two evenings out would probably equal all of them. But each time they hung up, Anne felt a renewed void.

Stephen had been gone two weeks by the time Anne finally finished her initial analysis, and she chose first thing Tuesday morning to present it to Tomlin.

He looked receptive, motioning for her to close the door as he buzzed for a pot of coffee. That was a good sign, she thought, taking the seat across from him.

"Well, at this point I do have an overall view," she told him. "And I sure see the need for lots of policies you don't have, Mr. Tomlin." She wanted to test the water before jumping in.

"Good! Let's hear them!"

She'd seen that "Let's clean the house!" expression on attorneys' faces before. But it always crumbled as soon as you suggested moving the pencil sharpener five inches.

Beginning with the fact that there was no sign-in procedure, which she'd been warned was required by state law in a firm of K&W's size, Anne spent a half hour slicing through point after point of sadly needed changes in staff resource management before Tomlin said anything.

"Do institute the sign-in sheet immediately, but I want to think about your other suggestions. With this many people, they're probably necessary, but...oh, dear," he finally sighed. "Life is so much simpler in a small office."

"Ah, well you haven't heard the bad news." Anne laughed, turning to another section of her notes. "Your benefit package is so up in the air that no one knows where they stand."

"Overall, how do we compare with other firms?"

"Badly."

Tomlin coughed. "Taking all your suggestions together, what would be the annual cost increase?"

"That would involve a little more time. I thought I'd run some of my thoughts by you and see how you like the basic ideas first. Then I could play with the costs to see how much each benefit totals."

"I see." He settled back. "Okay, run them by."

After an hour of discussing salary reviews, sick leave, vacations, personal time off and Christmas bonuses, Anne found herself totally at ease, chatting enthusiastically about her ideas.

When she finally left a pause, Tomlin took a deep breath. "My dear, I'd certainly hate to take you shopping."

Anne laughed at the expression of pain on his face, realizing that she'd met each of his arguments with ten reasons why he'd save money by spending it. Why did men always have trouble seeing how that worked?

"I'm almost done," she promised, leafing through her file. "There's a whole slew of little cute-type benefits that some of the large firms offer. Now these don't cost much, Mr. Tomlin, but they're great for morale." Ignoring his expression, Anne continued searching for the sheet she wanted.

"'Cute' benefits?" He looked beaten, but he was hanging in there admirably.

"Ah, here it is," she said. "Now here's one I really like! A secretary can take fifteen minutes off four lunch hours until she accumulates an hour. Then she can have an occasional two-hour lunch break to handle personal business or whatever. And it costs the firm nothing! Don't you just love it?"

Tomlin shook his head in bland agreement. "It's just darling," he said. "But when do these ladies do any work?" He was now cradling his chin in his hand, and she had the feeling he was no longer listening.

"Oh, they work hard, Mr. Tomlin. But you have to admit, legal secretaries are under a lot of pressure. This just gives them a little flexibility, that's all." Anne put her papers back in the file, thinking she'd better stop while she was ahead. "Besides, I think things like this are kind of a nice touch."

"Mmm. Yes, well, now that I see how your mind works, I'm no longer worried about tightening the ship, but rather pampering the crew! Good heavens, Anne, what about us poor partners paying for all these 'nice touches'!"

Anne laughed at his feeble attempt to look stern, then raised her finger in the air. "Oh! That reminds me—speaking of nice touches, the reception room! We really must have a weekly delivery of flowers on the table across from the elevator, Mr. Tomlin. It's so severe and serious looking out there."

He shook his head. "I suppose a little levity might help keep the partners from getting suicidal over the increased overhead you're proposing." That was a typical Tomlin way to describe flowers. "A little levity."

"Good! I'll start them today." Anne put the file under her arm, getting up to leave.

"Don't tell me you're finally through."

"Yep." She walked toward the door, and then paused before opening it. "Oh—and of course you wouldn't mind if each Friday night a different secretary could take the flowers home, would you?"

A stern look crossed Tomlin's face. "Anne, are you certain you aren't a lawyer? You have this way of *negotiating* things." But something about his grumbling had the opposite effect on Anne than what he might have hoped for. She'd won his respect, and she knew it.

"Do you want to write the memo regarding the sign-in sheets, or—"

"No, you go ahead." He sighed. "We might as well lay a little groundwork for the office manager to get taken a bit more seriously—by the attorneys, as well, I suppose."

"And I can throw in at least the occasional long lunch hour thing without the stamp of a partners' meeting?"

Tomlin shook his head. "That doesn't seem too offensive. But I'll have to discuss the rest with my partners, so don't make any hints or promises—only that we're looking at things in general."

"Thanks, Mr. Tomlin. I'll start working up costs and a proposal for the partners' meeting."

As she opened the door, Anne's eyes fell on the maroon Persian rug in Tomlin's office. It was similar to Stephen's.

Two weeks down and two to go, she thought, patting her file as she walked down the hall. Besides, the idea of putting together a benefit package out of nothing wasn't too shabby a way to pass the time for someone with her meager experience.

The only remaining concern was whether the rest of the partners would be as open to changes as Tomlin appeared. Attorneys were so shortsighted about their own businesses that Anne had often wondered if whoever had written "The Cobbler's Daughter Has No Shoes" was a financial manager married to a lawyer.

Anne was curious to see what kind of reaction would come from her memo. As soon as she'd called the florist to open an account for weekly service, she carefully worded the memo so she could get it circulated right away.

But she ended the day in a very aggravated mood. At all costs she hadn't wanted any misunderstandings over controls, but as feared, Cooper's long-time secretary was absolutely irate.

To Jean, the idea of being asked along with everyone else to sign in her arrivals and departures bordered on insult. She was unaccustomed to having anyone question her at all, and she very strongly hinted that Anne could content herself with supervising the file clerks if she wanted, but she had no business dabbling in the affairs of people who had been with one of the seed firms longer than Anne had been out of high school.

Anne could understand the woman's anger. After all, new regulations would put an end to her long absences whenever Cooper was out.

But when Stephen called that night, he just laughed off the problem. "So what?"

"So what? If I'm going to gain any credibility at all, I have to be able to expect even 'Ms Tut' to go along with the rules. I should have asked her if she also wanted to be exempt from any new benefits that might be coming."

"Well, you won't have to deal with her that long, so I wouldn't bother about it if I were you."

"Why, is she quitting?"

There was a short silence, and then Stephen laughed abruptly. "My! You *are* obsessive! I'd better call Trudy and warn her you're entrenching."

Oops. She'd been so caught up in her own thoughts that she hadn't realized the impact of what she'd said. Damn! Suddenly she felt that emptiness that came whenever she thought about what she wasn't telling Stephen. But like every other time that he'd referred to Anne's expected departure, she was impelled to change the subject. After all, Trudy hadn't decided anything officially, and surely things would find some way of working out by then. Besides, with the responsibility she was getting, she couldn't risk losing either Stephen or K&W at this early stage.

"Maybe I am a little on edge," she said. "I've been keeping myself as busy as I can, and the days go fast enough, but then I leave and the evenings just drag. Plus, every time I walk by your office the clock seems to move slower again. It's sort of two extremes in the same place."

"I'm glad to hear that," he said. "You've been so involved with work that I was getting worried you'd start forgetting me."

"Not a chance."

"Anne?"

"Hmm?"

"I miss you. I *really* miss you."

When Stephen's voice got soft and intimate everything in her melted, and suddenly nothing else mattered in the world.

THE NEXT DAY when Anne got out of the elevator after lunch, Tracy waved frantically as she gulped down a mouthful of coffee.

"Tomlin wants to see you right away. Something's wrong."

"Oh?" Anne's eyebrows raised in surprise. She didn't stop at her office to drop off her purse but went straight into his.

"I'm glad you're here," he said brusquely. "Close the door." He waited impatiently until she'd crossed the room to his desk.

"Stephen's in New York with dead files." Tomlin looked at her, expecting that she would join in his dismay.

"Wh—"

"*Dead files!*" He leaned across the desk, repeating the words as if he couldn't comprehend their meaning himself. "That young trainee that Butler hired sent Stephen with the wrong files! I can't believe that someone could Xerox a whole half drawerful of a sister case that's been settled for six months! She didn't bother to check the case number, of course."

He paced up and down his office, his face reddening with each step he took. "Stephen's sitting in New York, ready to go to Washington to try someone else's case, and he doesn't even have so much as the litigation clip."

Tomlin seemed to be trying to impress the reality on himself rather than on Anne, and she advanced a soft suggestion. "Can't we Xerox the right ones and send them by air carrier?"

He hadn't even heard what she'd said. "*Damn!* And of all clients . . ."

Suddenly he stopped and looked at her. "Anne, there's no room for any mistakes to be made with this client. They comprise a good fifth of the office caseload, and they're touchy. Very touchy. And particularly—most particularly—with regard to this matter. There have been three separate lawsuits filed, all among the same parties, and it's already incredibly messy."

He looked ready to explode. "How could anyone copy a whole half drawer of a case that's been settled for six months! And why was it still in her drawer?" he demanded.

Anne held up her hand to calm him. "Mr. Tomlin, an experienced secretary could if she wasn't here to see the sister case tried, let alone a trainee. So? We'll just fix it."

"I don't see how—" He was too upset to think.

"When is the trial?" she interrupted, hoping to get him off his rampage.

"Monday morning. In Washington."

"How many files are there?"

"About a half drawerful." He looked at Anne, and the darkness in his eyes told her why the staff was so worried about crossing him up. "Stephen has to review them all, and—"

"Okay, simple. This is Wednesday afternoon. I'll have them Xeroxed by tonight. I'll get one of the boys to stay.

"Tomorrow morning is Thursday," she continued. "I'll get them to an air carrier and have them to Stephen by tomorrow night. If he's just starting on them now, anyway, he'll only lose a day and a half."

Tomlin shook his head adamantly. "It's too late to take any chances," he said. "Once they leave our hands, they're in the hands of . . . *disinterested clerks!*"

She started to protest, but he interrupted, speaking more to himself than to her.

"At this point I want them hand delivered. By somebody who won't get on the wrong plane!"

Anne was watching a perfect sample of the paranoia she'd heard about. Surely the man couldn't be serious. But one look at him told her he was.

After a moment Tomlin's eyes slowly targeted on Anne. "How would you like to spend a weekend in New York?"

"*Me?*" Her voice croaked.

"Yes!" He almost sputtered. "Stop wasting time—can you take them? And *hand deliver* them to Stephen?" He stressed the words as though to be sure she understood he didn't mean air carrier—he meant Anne carrier.

"I . . . I guess so." Her mind raced, trying to take all this in as excitement began welling up in her throat. Stephen! She'd see Stephen!

"How long will it take to Xerox them?" he asked, his expression scheming.

Anne brought her attention back to the crisis. "If it's really half a drawer, it could take well into the night."

"And if the machine breaks down?" That was a valid concern. Machinery had a habit of doing just that at times like this.

"I could call our repairman and try to talk him out of his home number. He loves playing God when things get really rough."

Suddenly every muscle in Tomlin's delicate little body visibly relaxed. "So you'll book a flight first thing in the morning and come to the office early enough to make spot checks to be sure it's all there. You'll pick up the files and go to the airport. You'll get on the plane, and take them with you…as your carryon piece."

Anne kept quiet as he continued dry-running the minutest details. "Stephen's scheduled to go to Washington tomorrow at five-thirty their time. That's two-thirty our time. If you leave on the first flight out, you can get there with an hour or so to spare before his flight leaves. That'll allow for all but the most horrid delays."

His voice trailed to a mumble. "So they'll be in *your* hands until you intercept Stephen. Then they'll be in *his* hands. That'll give him Friday, Saturday and Sunday...and he should be prepared by Monday, yes?" Tomlin spun around, and his expression had the cast of a madman on a hot discovery.

"Yes," Anne assured, suppressing the giddy laugh that threatened to burst out. "I can get here in plenty of time, and I'll keep checking on its progress tonight. Nothing will go wrong."

Tomlin leaned forward and focused into her eyes with a deadly look. "Anne, this would be very embarrassing if it got out, particularly with this client—they just can't take a joke at all."

Anne laughed at his wry choice of words, but he continued with a look of admonishment, as though he hadn't meant it to be funny. "I don't want one word of this to get out—to anyone, you understand? Not even the Xerox people."

"I'll handle it very discreetly," Anne assured him, rising to leave. Suddenly she felt like a hit man who'd just been retained by the Mafia.

"Tomorrow and Friday you're out of the office...at some word processing demonstration," he added, putting on his glasses.

"Okay." She headed toward the closed door.

"And Anne?"

"Yes?"

"Fire her."

She turned, watching as he picked up a stack of correspondence to sign. "Oh, come on, Mr. Tomlin, she's just learning. Besides, anyone can make a mistake."

"Not a mistake like that, they can't." He was serious.

Anne debated for a moment. It could be dangerous in his mood, but she couldn't resist. "How about Butler in his tree?"

Tomlin slowly peered at her over his bifocals. He remained silent, but his expression told her she'd said just the right thing.

ANNE SPENT THE REST of the afternoon overseeing the Xeroxing. She had enlisted Sam, the most responsible, along with one of the other fellows to stick with the files till they were done. Predictably, Sam assumed it was just one more of Tomlin's rushes and crunched into it like a trooper.

As soon as Tomlin saw the whole thing under way, he stopped by Anne's office. He looked drained. "I have a golf weekend planned in Palm Springs. I was going to leave tomorrow at noon, but I'm starting to wonder if I should stay home—just in case there's any problem."

Anne was clearing off her desk. "Isn't that the tournament you mentioned earlier?"

"Yes, but—"

"Oh, for heaven's sake, Mr. Tomlin. Go!" It was like watching the mother of nine new pups torn between a much-needed trip into the yard and leaving the litter long enough to take it.

"I'll tell you what," she began, "my plane lands at four o'clock New York time, which is one o'clock our time. I'll call you the very second he gets the files—'in his hands,'" she added with a teasing grin. "Then you can go with a clear mind. However, if there's any hitch, then you can stay home and panic."

A slow smile of relief spread across Tomlin's face. "Anne, you're a wonderful girl. Did anyone ever tell you that?"

"Yes, Mr. Tomlin. As a matter of fact, yes." She gave him a wink, not quite trusting how he'd have reacted to the bear hug she felt like enveloping him in. *She was going to see Stephen!*

With Sam making steady progress on the files, Anne left at four-thirty to go home and pack. It was going to be an early morning.

She had no sooner closed the door to her apartment than the phone rang. She knew it would be Stephen.

"Hi. I'm told you're escorting the files."

"Isn't that a stroke?" Anne giggled, pulling the phone to the couch.

"It would be, except that I'm leaving at the same time." He sounded really disgusted.

"I know. But at least we can have coffee together."

"'We can have coffee together,'" he imitated sarcastically.

"Well, that's more than a telephone conversation." All Anne could think about was that she'd be in Stephen's arms two weeks earlier than she would have otherwise. For a few minutes, at least.

"That's true. It just makes me sick, though, not to be able to spend some time with you—especially in New York."

"My flight is scheduled out at eight o'clock. I'll be there at four, your time. And yours leaves at five-thirty, right?"

"At five-thirty, yes."

"Perfect, you see? So we *can* have coffee together!"

Stephen laughed, defeated. "I can't believe he won't trust an air carrier, and he's actually sending a live messenger to hand it to me personally."

"Oh, Stephen, he's so cute. I'm really getting excited. He said I should see the city while I'm there."

"He did?"

"Sure! There's no way I could get back on a flight tomorrow afternoon, and what's the point in flying home on a Friday? It was his idea—hotel is all paid for and everything."

"Dammit," he groaned. "I wish I could show it to you. But Friday night I'm scheduled to have dinner with cocounsel in Washington, and he's going to be out of town over the weekend, so there's just no way I can't be there. It's the only time I can confer with him prior to Monday."

Stephen sighed. "I've been trying to find some way to work this out. I called the airport already and asked how flights were on Friday morning, thinking I could stay and have dinner with you and at least take you to a show one night, anyway. But they're booked solid because of the weekend. I still can't believe not being able to get a one-hour flight from New York to Washington because of summer bookings, but she said it was unusually heavy."

"Well, you can't afford to take the chance of any more slipups. Mr. Tomlin would have a heart attack. Besides, you do have to review the files."

"I know. And there's always the idea of getting a phone call in Washington Friday and not having checked in yet."

"So we'll have coffee together," she reminded, her voice prompting him to brighten up.

"I guess you're right—it's better than a telephone call."

"Oh, Stephen, you should have seen Mr. Tomlin. He looked so . . . violent!"

"Well, she *should* have checked the case number. Anytime you have sister files or cross suits you double-check every document, let alone a whole drawerful of files. With an error of that magnitude, I'll bet he was fit to be tied. I certainly was."

"He wanted me to fire her."

Stephen paused. "Well, that's a little strong."

"I know. I was afraid he'd throw a book at me, but I re-minded him about Butler sawing himself out of a tree."

"You're kidding."

"Took the wind right out of his sails." She giggled again. "I think he's developing a fatherly affection toward you—he said you were 'refreshing.'"

Anne smiled to herself. "And what did you say?"

"Simply that I wanted to get you naked in the Xerox room." Stephen's raspy voice was filled with the pure lechery of a dirty old man.

Anne gasped. "Oh, God! Why do I always fall for these things?" She laughed at the picture in her mind. "And worse yet, why can I envision you really doing something like that to him—and me?"

"Oh, we torture him whenever we get the chance—it's the only way for him to know he's loved and appreciated. And as for you—"

"Typical," she said, deliberately cutting him off. "Oh, typical of lawyers."

Stephen laughed. "I will say one thing in all seriousness, though. He certainly seems to be developing some faith in your judgment, from the way he talks about you."

Anne blushed. "I'm flattered."

"No, you're bright. He doesn't trust anything to go right."

"Oh, Stephen, I just can't wait to see you."

She could hear his grin all the way across the line. "Keep saying things like that. It makes me feel like I'm not the only one who violates all semblance of sanity. Look, I'll get to the airport in plenty of time in case your flight arrives early. With a little luck we'll have enough time to slip into one of the storage lockers for an hour or so."

"Wait a minute—you'd better allow more time than that, you brute."

"For a short kiss? See you tomorrow."

8

THE VAST CITY PEEKED through little holes in the clouds, showing a landscape that was flat but jumbled, with buildings stuck in every possible corner. The plane made another circle.

Anne's heart seemed to be beating steadily yet slightly faster than normal as she listened to books getting stuffed into purses and briefcases snapping shut. Reaching for her own bag, she took one last glimpse in her tiny hand mirror. It revealed exactly what it had the last two times. She looked just fine.

Stowing her bag under the seat in front of her, Anne saw that the two accountant's cases were still there, just as they'd been through the whole flight, crammed as far as they would go under the pair of seats she occupied.

After another glance at her watch, she sat back and waited. Was this plane having to circle because the airport was that busy, or were there a bunch of guys down there, frantically running around with headsets on, trying to figure out which plane was supposed to be using which runway? In any event, if this plane was circling, were there others? Anne hated circling. Especially in clouds.

Finally the pilot announced that it was time to land. Anne's fingers absentmindedly stroked the loose end of the seat belt as she fixed her gaze once again outside the window.

Within moments the runway appeared just ahead. The ground was steadily getting closer and closer, and just as the wheels touched down, Anne's heart leaped. What if she heard the pilot scream, "Dammit, the brakes are out!"

She felt her fingers tighten on the armrests, her wrists bearing down with a steady pressure, as though she had a definite role in stopping the plane. Why did it always feel as if they were going to do a nosedive any minute? She hated landings.

As seat belts unsnapped, the man who had been nice enough to carry the huge briefcases aboard at the Los Angeles airport leaned forward, offering again.

Grateful, Anne let him take them to just inside the waiting room, insisting that she could handle them from there. After all, what were two broken arms pulled out of their sockets when a brown-eyed two-year-old was waiting to get hugged by her daddy?

Looking through the mass of faces, Anne saw Stephen behind a group of teenagers he couldn't penetrate. He waved at her, and she headed in his direction, lugging the two briefcases. She thought he had a strange expression on his face, but as she got closer she felt immediate concern. He looked pale.

"Hi, what's the matter?" She let the cases drop with a thud as she took his arm.

Stephen patted her hand. "I don't mean to be unceremonious, but my stomach is really acting up. You have the files?"

"Right here." She motioned to them, more interested in him.

He looked relieved, though definitely hazy. "Let's sit you and them down." Walking with her toward the seats in the waiting area, Stephen placed the files next to a chair. "I'll be back in a minute."

Anne sat down and waited, worrying about how pallid he was. Just when she was starting to wonder if he was all right, he returned, looking even worse. "Stephen, are you okay?"

"I think I'll be fine. I started feeling a little dizzy on my way to the airport, and then it got worse while I was waiting for your flight."

Anne noticed tiny beads of perspiration on his forehead. "Let's go into the restaurant and get you some soda crackers and 7-Up. That settles anything."

"Good idea," he agreed. "I've heard that's the best thing for an upset stomach."

Anne lifted the heavy accountant's cases, but Stephen took them from her. "Here, I'm not that sick." His grin was uncharacteristically feeble.

"Oh, I almost forgot," Anne said. "I promised Mr. Tomlin—"

"Phone's right here," he interrupted. Like a robot he guided her toward the pay booth, taking a seat just across the aisle.

Anne placed the call, turning to look at Stephen as she waited for the connection. He seemed barely awake. As soon as she was able to hang up from the short conversation, she quickly headed toward him. "Stephen, you really don't look well at all."

"I'll be fine. Let's get some crackers." He groaned to a standing position.

They made their way to the restaurant, which fortunately wasn't too far away, because Stephen was walking unsteadily.

After Anne had placed the order, Stephen settled back in the booth. "I don't know what it could be," he said. "I've never felt so dizzy." He closed his eyes, and Anne took his hand. It was dry and hot.

"Stephen, what did you eat today?"

He didn't respond. He was asleep.

"Stephen," she urged, shaking him.

He stirred. "I'm sorry, I must have dozed off. I'm having trouble . . . staying awake." He closed his eyes again.

Anne put her hand on his forehead. "Stephen," she insisted, shaking him, "what did you have to eat today?"

"Bacon and eggs for breakfast, a fish salad for lunch—"

"A fish salad? Where?"

"A little coffee shop down the street from the hotel," he answered slowly.

"Oh, no." She recognized the signs. "Stephen, I think you have food poisoning."

"I'm just so dizzy...if I can just go to sleep for a minute, I'm sure I'll be fine." His voice trailed off.

The waitress came with the order, and Anne asked for the check. She broke open the package of crackers, trying to make Stephen eat a couple of them along with a few sips of the 7-Up, but all he wanted was to close his eyes.

Anne felt his forehead again and shook him awake. "Stephen, you're not getting on any plane. I'm taking you back to my hotel, and I'm going to call a doctor. I'm just positive you have food poisoning."

"Okay," he agreed weakly. From what she'd seen of Stephen Merrifield, that wasn't a good sign.

"Can you walk?"

"Sure," he said as he rose from the booth, almost staggering.

Anne got a porter to carry the cases, asking if there was a wheelchair anywhere nearby.

"No, I can walk," Stephen argued. "As long as I'm up and moving, I'm fine."

The porter looked at Stephen and then paused for a moment. "Come with me," he said. "There's a shortcut that isn't open to the public. It ain't pretty, but it'll get you to a taxi a whole shade quicker."

Anne shot him a grateful look and followed through a back hallway, holding Stephen's arm. "Tell me if you think you're going to pass out or anything, Stephen."

He gave her a weak smile, seeming to concentrate all his effort on walking.

As soon as they got outside, the porter hailed a taxi, which pulled up to the curb.

"Oh! My luggage!" Anne gasped. It was probably riding around on a conveyer belt somewhere.

"No sweat, I'll get it," said the porter, holding out his hand. As Anne fumbled in her purse for the ticket envelope, he turned to the driver. "Pull over there into the loading zone and wait—I won't be long."

When he was gone the taxi driver shot a suspicious glance at Stephen.

"He has food poisoning," Anne explained quickly.

"Sure, lady," he said, turning back toward the front of the cab. He looked bored.

Suddenly it dawned on Anne that Stephen's luggage was probably destined for Washington without him. "Stephen! *Your* luggage!"

He reached into his breast pocket and pulled out his tickets, moving like an automaton, and then he went back to sleep.

When the porter returned with both of Anne's suitcases, she explained about Stephen's. "Is there any way you could retrieve it and have it delivered to the hotel?"

He looked at his watch. "I'll give it a good try," he said. "Meanwhile you better get this cat to a doctor."

Anne told him the name of her hotel and wrote her name on the back of Stephen's claim check, pushing it into the porter's hand along with a twenty-dollar bill. "I'm really trusting you," she said. This was all happening too fast.

He looked at the bill. "Well, thank you, ma'am." Then his expression became earnest, and kind old eyes met hers reassuringly. "Don't need to worry none. I been here a long time."

When they got to the hotel Anne left Stephen in the cab while she checked in. The desk clerk said there was a general practitioner nearby who acted as their house doctor, and he'd call him immediately.

Ten minutes of bellboy, elevator and hallways found them in Anne's room, and Stephen headed straight for the bed, collapsing on it, jacket and all. Then, almost in the same motion, he got back up and staggered into the bathroom.

When he emerged he dropped heavily onto the bed and closed his eyes. "This is all I need." He grimaced.

Anne felt his head again. "I'm just sure it's food poisoning, Stephen. I've had it before, and it was exactly like this." Not knowing what else to do, she went into the bathroom for a cold washcloth and placed it on Stephen's forehead. She saw a faint smile cross his lips before he fell asleep.

Within moments there was an abrupt knock at the door. Anne opened it to find a middle-aged man, still in his office smock with a stethoscope around his neck. He had a fat black leather kit bag in his hand.

"Ms Michaels? I'm Dr. Weinstock." He had an efficient voice and a competent demeanor.

"I'm glad you got here so fast," said Anne, moving aside to let him in.

Dr. Weinstock gently shook Stephen awake and asked him all the expected questions, taking his temperature and flashing lights in his eyes. He certainly seemed to know what he was doing. Anne trusted him immediately.

Finally he turned to her as Stephen drifted back into his haze. "You're a good diagnostician, Ms Michaels."

"How long do you think he'll be sick?"

He shrugged as he began repacking his kit. "No way to tell, but I don't think he's too bad off. I use a pretty good remedy. I'll call it down to the hotel pharmacy and have it delivered. It tastes abominable, but it's a miracle. Give it to him every two hours all night, and by tomorrow morning he should be feeling better."

"And if he's asleep?"

Dr. Weinstock looked up as though Anne had said something amusing. "Wake him." Closing his bag, he handed her a card with his night number encircled. "I'll stop in tomorrow morning and look at him again."

"Fine," said Anne, seeing him out.

"Oh, one more thing," he added, pausing in the hallway. "Don't open your door the way you did."

"No?"

"This is New York. Always ask who it is first."

"Oh. Certainly. Thanks so much." She closed the door, letting him hear her lock it.

Walking slowly back to Stephen's bed, Anne inspected the hotel room at the same time. A very serious-looking radiator stood under each of two windows, and the windows themselves were covered by pull-down shades, with fixed drapes on each side. Austere but certainly comfortable enough.

Stephen looked so peaceful and oblivious. It was interesting how one absolutely "had to catch a plane," until a little food poisoning reduced the "had" to a "couldn't." But assuming that the doctor was right about his feeling better by tomorrow, she'd better make some calls to see what she could do about getting him to Washington. If not by plane, then maybe by car.

Glancing at her watch to mark the time, Anne headed for one of the windows to peer through the slit. "Mmm, lovely," she said, looking at the side of a tan brick building. *No wonder they keep the shades drawn.*

The phone rang. The luggage had gone on, the porter told her. But at least the information was definite, and she could start working things out from there.

After a half hour of talking with the airline and one very chatty pharmacy delivery girl, Anne was again at Stephen's bedside, armed with a plastic vial of something that smelled like liquid chalk.

"Come on," she softly urged, "wake up."

Raising himself up seemed to take all Stephen's effort, but somehow he looked absolutely lovable in his vulnerable state. "I don't know if I can swallow something that even the doctor called awful. I really feel nauseated as it is."

Anne smiled understandingly, but she held the medicine out to him, trying not to laugh at the dread on his face. "Oh, come on, give it a try," she coaxed. "If you remember, the doctor also said it was a terrific remedy. A miracle, no less."

Stephen propped himself up on one elbow, drinking only half the measured dose before his face contorted into an involuntary grimace. Shaking his head, he tried to hand it back to her.

"Oh, no, you don't. Take it all."

His expression told her she was asking the impossible, but he downed the rest, reaching for the glass of water she'd brought. *"Dammit!"* he rasped. *"That's disgusting!"*

"How are you feeling?"

"Same as before. How long have I been sleeping?"

"About forty-five minutes. Do you feel awake enough to talk?"

"Sure. What's the matter?" he asked wearily.

"Well, I've been on the phone, and your luggage went to Washington. The porter couldn't get it off the plane."

She shushed his curse. "I called the airport, and they'll hold it for you in D.C."

"Fine," he said, shrugging.

"The reservations clerk said you'd probably have a pretty good chance of getting a standby flight, so that seemed another reason to leave it."

"That's good news." He looked as though he was barel
awake, but she continued, anyway.

"Meanwhile the suit you're wearing is all you've got at th
moment, so I called the front desk, and there's a little men'
shop right down the way. If you think you'll be all right alon
for a few minutes . . ."

"Yes, go," he mumbled. "Shaving cream, toothbrush . . .
His voice trailed off.

"Stephen, are you sure you'll be all right?"

"Yes, I'm fine, really. Just sick, that's all."

"That makes no sense whatsoever," she said. But he'd al
ready begun to doze off.

Almost running down the street, Anne noticed the shop
were beginning to close for the day. But the men's store wa
right around the corner as promised, and the salesman,
gem.

He was just closing himself, he apologized, but after hear
ing Anne's story he stepped aside with a flourish of wel
come.

They spent a moment comparing Stephen's build to var
ious men they saw on the street, with Anne adding a little her
and there. "I know just the type," he said, going back inside
Relying on his knowledge of sizes, Anne picked out socks an
briefs and finally asked for something comfortable to slee
in. There were some lounge pajamas on sale that were com
fortable looking, in a light cotton blend. For twenty dollars
they were a steal.

On the way back to the hotel, Anne caught sight of an odd
looking little market across the street. A quick detou
brought the reward of the basic toiletries Stephen woul
need, along with the bonus of a box of soda crackers and
six-pack of 7-Up. Anne was convinced the combination coul
cure anything short of terminal lice.

Riding up in the elevator, she looked at her watch, amazed. The whole trip had taken just over thirty minutes, and she had everything she'd hoped to find. Now all she wanted was to make sure he was all right, and to take off her shoes.

But as the door opened Anne laughed at the sight of Stephen sleeping in a rigid position, undoubtedly trying not to wrinkle his suit.

"Stephen," she called, setting down the packages, "wake up. I have some 7-Up and crackers and a really comfortable-looking surprise." She reached for the bag from the men's store, unfolding the loungies for him to see.

He squinted. "Oh, great." It was a weak reply, and he didn't look as if he wanted to move.

"Come on." She placed her hands behind his broad shoulders. "I'll help you." There was no way she'd be able to lift him, so the gesture was more of a coax than anything.

But finally he was sitting. "This is like having no strength at all."

"Oh, it'll get better once you get something reasonable in your stomach. I'll have to wake you again in a little while to take more medicine, but you'll sleep much better in these."

Laying the pajamas in Stephen's lap, Anne pulled his tie off and then began unbuttoning his shirt. As her knuckles brushed against the soft hair on Stephen's chest, she caught herself in a blush of self-reproach. Here the poor man was practically dying, and what was she thinking?

Suddenly Stephen gently pushed her out of the way as he went into the bathroom, lounge pajamas still in hand.

Shaking her head in sympathy, Anne kicked off her shoes as she dug into the market bag. After prying everything out of impossible wrappers, she bundled the supplies into the bag, calling through the bathroom door that she was leaving them there.

As she was pulling down the covers, the door opened momentarily, and Stephen mumbled an almost inaudible "Thanks." Then came the familiar, universal chick-a-chick of teeth being brushed.

Anne grinned as she fluffed the pillows. *He shaves, she showers. He brushes his teeth, she puts in her contacts. Puppies in a box. Just like puppies in a box. I'll bet Trudy would just die.*

The sound of a light clicking off made Anne glance up from pouring him a glass of 7-Up. "Lord, Stephen, do you have to look so incredibly sexy in them?" Sick or not, he was gorgeous.

Stephen arched an eyebrow, somehow able to appreciate the irony for the two seconds it took him to spot the open bed. Then, flopping into it, he was asleep before she even had time to offer him the drink, let alone the crackers.

Taking a sip herself, Anne went into the bathroom to retrieve Stephen's suit and shirt from the various knobs and hooks where he'd discarded them. After putting everything on carefully spaced hangers, she unpacked her own suitcase, pulling out some jeans, a T-shirt, her slippers and a book. It would be a long evening, all right. Reading, television and dinner à la room service. At least she'd have five minutes of company once every two hours, she mused.

But by ten-thirty, affected by the combination of stress and very little sleep the night before, Anne found herself nodding off.

Snapping off the television, she headed for the bathroom to get ready for bed before Stephen's next dose. This time she'd get him to eat a soda cracker, at least.

With her face scrubbed to a shine, Anne padded across the room, filling the vial as she called Stephen's name.

The light from the bed table cast a warm glow on the soft brushed cotton of her gown, and instead of the grimace she'd expected, Stephen made an approving sweep over her with his eyes. "This is a fine note," he said weakly. "Here I am not only in New York with you—which I'd said I couldn't manage—but I'm in bed, and you're still standing."

"Aw, come on, Stephen—don't you think it's time to stop the sick act?" Anne laughed at his expression, holding out the plastic dispenser.

"Oh, what I wouldn't give," he said, now accustomed to downing it in one gulp. Handing it back to her, he lay back. "My head feels about ten feet wide."

Anne felt his forehead. He didn't look quite as pale and maybe a touch more alert. "Are you feeling any better at all?" Her voice came out all soft and caring.

Stephen swallowed, still looking very weak. "I think so. At least I can talk straight. I felt almost drunk before." Suddenly he shaded the light from his eyes and squinted up at her, taking in the nightgown. "You sleeping with me?" His hair was rumpled, and there was a grin on his face.

Anne laughed slightly. "No choice. There's only one bed."

"Good," he sighed. His eyes fell closed, and there was a peaceful look on his face as he patted the space next to him. He was already drifting off.

AS THE NIGHT WENT ON Stephen seemed a little more lucid on each awakening, yet he continued to refuse to eat, wearing out after only a few minutes of talking. Between doses Anne tried to disturb him as little as possible, but she was amused to note that each time the alarm went off, she'd find herself curled up against him. It seemed like the most natural thing in the world.

At last she became vaguely aware of horns beeping somewhere in the distance, then footsteps in the hall. Ignoring the intrusions, she snuggled closer, just awake enough to enjoy the warmth of the body next to her yet sleepy enough not to want to move quite yet.

About to drift off to sleep again, Anne abruptly realized what those intruding noises meant, and she sat up. "Stephen! I forgot to set the alarm! It's morning!"

Pushing the hair out of her eyes, she reached for the little white travel clock. "Ten o'clock!" she groaned. "It's been six hours!" Anne started to fumble with the covers, but a strong hand covered her shoulder.

The sureness of Stephen's grip seemed out of place, and she turned to see the smile that slowly spread over his face. The life had come back into his complexion, and he looked rested and well.

"What an angel," he whispered, looking at the unruly wave of light brown hair that kept falling over one eye.

Anne pushed it aside once again, wondering if she looked anywhere near as disheveled as she felt. "You're feeling better?" Her voice had the huskiness it always had first thing in the morning.

Stephen took a deep breath that slowly developed into a yawn, pulling every muscle in his body into a long, hard stretch. "Ah, thanks to you," he said, letting all the air out at once. Then he scratched his head. "Still not perfect but definitely on the mend." His old voice was back.

"How's your head?"

Stephen paused a moment. "Now that still hurts."

"Do you feel like being sick or—"

"No," said Stephen. "I think all I need at this point is another fifteen hours of you snuggled up next to me." He pulled her down to him once again.

Relieved, Anne slid back under the covers, burrowing her face into Stephen's chest as he leisurely stroked her hair. "Mmm, and not even a single soda cracker," she said

"I didn't have the heart to tell you this, sweetie, but I hate soda crackers. Do you have stock in Nabisco?"

"No, I just know that they settle—"

There was an abrupt tap at the door, and Stephen's movements stopped.

"That's Dr. Weinstock," said Anne, recognizing the authoritative knock.

Though her gown was modest enough, Stephen told her to go into the bathroom—he'd answer it.

On the way Anne grabbed a jump suit from the closet, thinking she might as well take her shower while Stephen was getting the AMA stamp of approval.

By the time she returned, the doctor had gone and Stephen was sitting at the table glancing through one of the files. He'd poured himself a glass of 7-Up.

"The good doctor is as amazed as a proud father, and I can eat anything within reason," he announced. His gaze slid from her toes to her hips to her breasts and finally to her amused eyes.

"You certainly look hungry," said Anne, blushing slightly as she pulled the brush through her hair in unhurried strokes.

"That I am. I hope you like English muffins, because there are two of them coming up this very minute, along with a pot of coffee—and some orange juice for you."

"Anything," she agreed. "The coffee's the important thing as far as I'm concerned—I need my fix before I can function."

Stephen watched for a few minutes as the waves became more organized with each stroke. Finally a half smile tilted the corners of his mouth. "That was *not* my idea of how to spend the night with a beautiful lady, by the way."

Anne laughed. "I cuddled up with you all night, anyway."

"I know. That was what made me get better—to hell with that disgusting medicine." Stephen reached across the table to take her hand, and she noticed the slightly sheepish smile on his face. "Well, no one can say we're strangers any longer." The slightest reddening in his complexion was accompanied by a wry laugh. "How to get to know someone in a hurry. Get sick in her room, send her out for underwear and wake her every two hours to feed you medicine." He shook his head.

Anne held her brush in midair. "Oh, come on. You aren't bothered by that, are you?"

Stephen arched an eyebrow. "Well, it probably won't stand out as one of my most boastful memories."

"Well, *I'm* not bothered by it," she said, shooting him a look of reproach. That seemed to put him at ease.

After breakfast Stephen was still a little weak, but he decided to take a shower and shave. "Just for the fun of it," he said. But Anne could tell he was beginning to think about going to the airport. He had that pondering look.

TWO HOURS LATER she found herself looking out from a window at Kennedy Airport. As Stephen's plane grew smaller and smaller in the distance, she felt more alone than she'd ever imagined possible.

For a moment she considered returning to the hotel just long enough to pack before leaving herself. But in the next instant she knew she'd regret that. Going back to Los Angeles wouldn't make her feel any better than a weekend of sight-seeing in New York.

But Bloomingdale's, Greenwich Village, the Statue of Liberty and Central Park—even the Fifth Avenue Presbyterian Church on Sunday morning—didn't seem quite the way they would have with Stephen by her side.

9

WHEN ANNE RETURNED to the office Monday morning, Tomlin was as happy as could be. Not only had he done well in his tournament, but the files had been delivered without a hitch. There was no question about Stephen's delayed arrival in Washington, so that little concern became past history.

THE NEXT TWO WEEKS were filled with violent ups and downs for Anne. From nine to five she was in her glory. Every free moment was spent working on her benefit-cost analysis, and Tomlin gave her more and more responsibility with every day that passed. He included her in things that showed trust in her discretion, and he asked her about matters that indicated respect for her opinion. He was a fatherly soul, and Anne was beginning to enjoy him immensely.

But as fast as the days flew, the nights dragged by. On the few evenings when she didn't hear from Stephen, Anne went to bed feeling like a child who'd been stood up at the gates of Disneyland. Gone were any prudent thoughts that his absence would give her time to think. New York had fixed that. She was in love with Stephen Merrifield at his worst, as well as his best.

FINALLY THE DAY CAME when Stephen was to return. Anne resisted the urge to wear anything that wasn't part of her usual work wardrobe, but she chose the taupe suit with a cream silk blouse and her three-strand gold chain necklace. That seemed a fair compromise.

She was on the litigation side when he arrived and, of all things, standing right at Eileen's desk, picking up some overflow tapes for Mable. Anne hadn't wanted to be there when Stephen came in, but there was no mistaking his arrival.

"Honey, I'm home!" he bellowed. He was still somewhere down the hall.

Typewriters stopped momentarily as Anne's hand flew to her mouth, her eyes darting to Eileen's. But clucking like an old mother hen, the older woman giggled delightedly. "There he is, shy as always. He did that to me once before, and the chairman of the board of a very stodgy client nearly dropped his spectacles."

Relieved, Anne's heart nevertheless began to flutter as swift, heavy footsteps grew nearer.

She watched as Stephen rounded the partition wall and immediately plunked a little wrapped box onto Eileen's desk. "For you, my sweet." He was exuberant. And absolutely beautiful.

"Oh, Stephen, you shouldn't have," Eileen reprimanded him.

"Well, Anne! Good to see you!" he exclaimed in the hearty tone of a politician on the campaign trail, but the way he rolled his eyes said just what Anne wanted to hear.

There was still a grin on her face left over from his unorthodox entrance. "This is *definitely* the looser side of the office," she responded with a laugh.

Eileen glanced up from admiring the box. "At least it is since Stephen came with the firm. It used to be rather... 'uptight.'" She chose the phrase as if trying it on for the first time, giggling a little as she returned to the task of unwrapping her present. "Oh, Stephen, you shouldn't have," she scolded again.

Stephen's eyes met Anne's with brazen directness as Eileen immersed herself in struggling with the ribbon. "I love you," he mouthed silently, his eyebrows drawn together in an expression of longing.

A deep blush rose to Anne's face, and she made a fast attempt to fill in the loud silence Stephen was leaving. "How was your flight back?" She couldn't believe he'd said that.

"Better with every mile. God, am I glad to be home!" He looked at Anne meaningfully before finally calling on discretion. Turning into his office, he snapped on the light as he rounded the corner. "Eileen! Can I have some coffee?"

Just then Eileen extricated the box from its wrapping and opened it. "Oh, Stephen! It's beautiful!" she exclaimed. It was a lovely little gold pin of the White House.

"Well, if I can't take my secretary to D.C., then I can damned well bring D.C. to my secretary!" he called. "Say, Eileen, I have an idea. Pin it on that sexy blouse on the way to the coffee room!"

"*Stephen Merrifield!*" she gasped, her eyes flying to Anne's. "He observes no rules of etiquette whatsoever," she explained, getting to her feet.

Anne shook her head as the two women walked toward the reception room, touched and amused by the blush that was still on Eileen's cheeks. "That Stephen—" Eileen chuckled "—he sure knows how to win a woman's heart."

Anne laughed understandingly, resisting all comments that came to mind. "He must think a lot of you," she said. With an affectionate pat on the older woman's shoulder, she watched as Eileen bustled proudly into the coffee lounge to display her pin.

Anne glanced at her watch as she continued on toward Tomlin's office. Three o'clock. Not much longer to wait. . . .

Mable was deep in concentration, counting pages of exhibits when Anne approached. Looking up, the small, wiry woman gave her nod of appreciation when she saw the finished work, yet her mouth never stopped its silent tally.

"Hello, Anne," called Tomlin, seeing her outside.

She popped her head through the door. "Merrifield's back."

"Oh, good!" He clasped his hands together. "Mable," he called, "make another reservation for dinner—I want Stephen to meet them, too!"

Anne's heart sank.

"New client." He chortled as he picked up the phone and dialed Stephen's extension.

"Stephen, my boy! How was your flight?" He yelled as if Stephen were still across the country. "I'm having dinner with Markson and two of the directors. I thought I'd have you join us."

He smiled as he listened to Stephen's reply. "Oh certainly," he continued. "I'll bet you are...." He covered the mouthpiece with his hand and whispered to Anne. "Tell her to cancel the extra reservation— What?" He directed his attention back to Stephen.

Anne turned to Mable. "Cancel, please. Merrifield can't make it." She grinned all the way back to her office.

No sooner had she entered her door than her phone rang. She had known it would. "Anne Michaels," she said officially.

"You're incredible." Stephen's voice was soft.

"So are you," she whispered.

"I'm going to settle a few quick things and then leave. How soon can you get out of here?"

"Anytime after five, as far as I can see now."

"Great. I'm going to have Eileen take me home. I'll leave about four-thirty. You leave around five-fifteen and meet me at my place."

"Okay."

"I want to take a shower and then we'll drive up the coast for dinner. God, I missed you," Stephen whispered.

"Me too." It was all she could say with one of the Xerox boys popping into her office. He fumbled through his cart for Anne's slot, plunking a stack of mail and memos in her In box.

Stephen figured as much. "Do you remember how to get to my place?"

"Yes."

"I'll see you, then."

TWO AND A HALF HOURS LATER Anne pulled onto Stephen's street, and her heart began to flutter. Remembering the last time she'd been there, she reflected with irony on how much her life had changed since that night. She parked her car in the street and walked up the driveway.

As soon as Anne rang the bell, a huge Siamese cat appeared from the bushes and rubbed the length of its body against her legs, wrapping its tail around her ankle before turning for another pass.

"Oh, vicious puddy tat," she said as it purred sleepily. Without the air conditioning of the office or her car, Anne began to realize what a hot day it had been.

Suddenly she heard striding footsteps cross a tile floor, and the cat prepared to leap through the door as soon as Stephen opened it.

He looked at Anne for a moment, as though she'd been lost forever, and the next thing she knew she was inside.

Closing the door with one arm and surrounding Anne with the other, Stephen covered Anne's lips with his in a starved kiss, long overdue. Without breaking from it, he took her purse from her hand and threw it across the room. She heard it land softly on a big overstuffed sofa as her arms went around his neck.

"Oh, did I miss you—" Stephen said in a muffled voice, unwilling to pull away from her lips enough to talk. Anne was just as intoxicated by the same feeling, that she'd never get enough of him.

After a long, lingering moment, Stephen held her a little away from him. "Let me just look at you," he said. His eyes searched her face adoringly. "I can't believe this long, stupid trip is over." He gathered her back into his arms again.

"Me neither, Stephen. I've never had time pass so unbelievably slowly." Strong back muscles rippled under her hands as she pressed her face against his chest. "This has been the most torturous month of my entire life."

Stephen laughed softly. "Ah, mine, too, but remember, I'm ten years older."

After they'd satisfied themselves that they weren't going to be separated if they got two feet away from each other, Stephen put his arm around her and guided her past well-preserved antiques into a large brick kitchen. On the breakfast bar were two glasses of wine already poured into chilled glasses, with little droplets of water around the bases.

"Are you hungry?"

"Not very. I had a late lunch."

"Good! I'm not either—for food." Stephen nodded toward the sliding glass door. "Let's go sit out on the patio for a while. It's too good to be home to leave quite yet, anyway."

Armed with his glass and some cocktail napkins, Stephen led the way onto a covered patio with fuchsias and ferns hanging everywhere. It was like another room, fully furnished with overstuffed wicker pieces and rattan tables. The only difference was the lack of walls, and the floor was brick instead of the tile and hardwood inside.

An old-fashioned glass wind chime tinkled in the breeze, and beyond the patio was a thick carpet of lawn surrounding a pool that looked very inviting at that moment. Air-conditioned offices made summer days come and go too fast.

Anne handed Stephen her glass so she could shed her jacket. "How is it that your plants, cat and house all look like someone's been home taking care of them?"

"I have a housekeeper," he said. "She comes once a week, but she stops in every day while I'm gone."

"It's so . . . lovely." Anne glanced at the wind chime again, draping her jacket over a chair. "It's certainly a far cry from the way you'd expect a bachelor to live."

"Home is pretty important to me," said Stephen, guiding her to the patio sofa. As soon as he sat down he draped his arm across the back of her seat, putting his feet up on the coffee table to relax.

Anne kicked her shoes off and joined him. "I was in Mr. Tomlin's office when he asked you to dinner. I almost died when I heard what he was up to."

"Not a chance, pretty lady." Stephen laughed softly as he curled a strand of her hair between his fingers.

Anne's eye was suddenly caught by the rose garden across the lawn. She shook her head, amazed once more. "What a truly beautiful yard this is! How can you stand to leave it for months at a time?"

Stephen groaned. "I can't. I'm so sick of traveling and eating in restaurants that I can't see straight." He took a sip of his wine.

"Hmm," he continued, plunking his glass on the table, "now there's a thought. What would you say to passing on driving up the coast for dinner? If I run to the store for some steaks and salad makings, I could barbecue while you slice."

A conspiratorial smile lit Anne's face. She didn't want to be stuck with a table between them all evening any more than he did. "You're on. I make a pretty mean salad, and I can't think of anything I'd like more."

"Me neither. I'm really sick of restaurant food."

"I'll bet you are." She laughed, thinking of New York.

"Mmm." He nodded, nuzzling his nose into her hair. "Do you have any comfortable clothes in the car?"

Anne dropped her head against his arm. "Oh, damn!" She usually kept a pair of jeans and a top in the trunk, but she'd cleaned the car out, and everything was in a laundry basket to be reorganized.

"Fear not, fair lady. I'll be right back," he said, getting up.

Stephen vanished into the house and returned within moments with a light cotton madras lounge robe. "A gift from my father on a trip to India," he said, amused. "It was way too small to begin with, but after it got mixed up in the wash, it met its final, sad fate in the clothes dryer." He held it out as if it were a dainty slip, whisking it back and forth in a dramatic display.

"Perfect!" said Anne, laughing at his antics. "It's just like those one-size-fits-all things that sells for forty dollars."

"It's yours!" He threw it to her with a flourish. "If we're staying home, I'm going to throw on a pair of shorts and a loose shirt, and I'd hate to think of you all bundled up in a business suit." He looked at his watch. "Actually, I'd better run down to the market first. The guy has the audacity to close at six-thirty, but he has the best steaks in the world, and they start disappearing fast about this time of day."

Anne got up. "Maybe I'll take a shower while you're gone. It's certainly hotter than I thought it would be." Her silk blouse was beginning to feel sticky against her back.

Stephen took her hand and planted a kiss on her cheek as they walked into the house. "Oh, it's so damned good to be home!" He punched the counter as they walked by.

Shortly after Stephen had left Anne stepped into a beautifully tiled shower, a large baggie pinned around her head. As she stood there for several moments under the rush of cool water, her eyes wandered to the windowsill. Funny, she'd never gazed upon a bottle of shampoo with loving affection before.

Stepping onto a plush bath mat, Anne quickly toweled dry before trying on the hoppi-style robe. From what she could see in the half-length mirror, it fitted surprisingly well, the thin fabric conforming to her body. It was a simple wrap with drop sleeves and a waist tie, and it came to about four inches above her knees. What could his father have been thinking? She laughed, picturing Stephen in it. But she was grateful for the miscalculation.

Anne hung her towel over the door and went into the living room for her purse. On her way back to the bathroom, she tentatively peered into each room.

The whole house was filled with a conglomeration of collectibles, along with serious antiques. There were objects d'art covering all available wall space, and a collection of the most interesting rugs were scattered over hardwood floors.

In Stephen's room was the full-length mirror Anne had hoped to find. Hoppi coats could look clumsy if the gathers weren't just right, and after all, vanity prevailed when one was twenty-nine and in love.

More than satisfied with the fit, Anne headed toward the door. But noticing an arrangement of family photographs on the wall, she stopped to look at them.

A wonderful-looking older couple occupied the center place, and even in advanced age the man looked very much like Stephen. The woman looked like someone who baked all the time and told great stories.

Anne's eyes fell to a box of more photographs on the dresser; jammed in sideways was a large glossy of an unusually beautiful young woman in her early twenties. Only the head showed, but it was the expression on her face that caught Anne's curiosity. Sheer ecstasy

Sliding it out just slightly revealed a flowing ballet costume, and Anne knew this had to be Cathy. It was an action shot, catching her in the middle of a performance.

Standing on pointe, she had magnificent form. Every finger was held perfectly, and her legs were clearly those of a dedicated dancer. She looked to be in absolute heaven.

For some reason Anne thought of the sadness in Stephen's eyes when he had said Cathy had moved back to Boston to open a ballet school for children. What could possibly be sad about that? Replacing the photo with an odd sense of reverence, Anne returned to the bathroom to brush her hair and add a few touches of makeup before heading back out to the kitchen.

How wonderful it felt to pad around on a cold tile floor in the summertime! Plunking her purse on the counter, Anne began a search for paring knives, cutting boards and a salad bowl. Stephen's housekeeper must be a gem, she thought as she located everything, piece by piece. Even the cabinets were immaculate.

With salad utensils in order, Anne stepped outside long enough to retrieve her wineglass. Dropping a few ice cubes into it, she settled onto a bar stool, wanting to take in the details of Stephen's kitchen while she waited.

The room was filled with plants and just enough friendly clutter to make it feel cozy and lived in. An interesting array of old gadgets and antique pots and pans adorned the walls near the cooking area, while modern prints mixed with old ones took care of the remaining wall space. The eclectic combination fitted Stephen's personality perfectly.

When Anne heard a car pull into the garage, she jumped up and opened the kitchen door to see if she could help. Stephen's dark eyes met hers through the tinted windshield for a long moment and then traveled down her body before he finally opened the car door. "That robe sure couldn't have met a better fate," he said, unfolding himself from the Lincoln.

Once the grocery bags were on the counter, he turned to Anne and caught her to him in a gentle hug. "It's pretty nice having you at the door when I pull into my garage."

Anne smiled, pressing her cheek against his chest. "That's good, because I can't imagine anyone I'd rather be opening doors for."

"Hmm. Now that has some kinky possibilities."

"Cook!" she ordered, laughing.

Stephen glanced at the salad setup. "Great! You've found your way around the kitchen—I hate it when people pussyfoot around, afraid to touch things."

"Yes, well, you certainly have an interesting supply of cooking utensils." She motioned to the wall. They were ancient, and she didn't know what half of them were for.

Stephen laughed at the expression on her face. "Ah, that's my private collection—old, weird things that someone threw out in favor of modern metal. I'm keeping them for posterity. See? Some of them I even use." He reached for a contraption, and Anne could tell he was about to impress her with some amazing accomplishment.

Stephen pulled out a bottle of California Chianti he'd bought at the store. "Here's a case where we've outdone the Italian originals," he said.

Anne watched him insert wnat looked like the very first attempt at a corkscrew. After watching him struggle for a few minutes, she looked at him lamely as he proceeded to chew the cork into shreds and crumbles with the antique.

"It worked before," he complained.

"When you're ready to give up, a high-heeled shoe and a hammer work wonders."

Stephen continued working at it. "The table outside is broken. Want to have a picnic in the shade under the walnut tree?" Another chunk of mangled cork fell.

Anne leaned across the counter, sadistically enjoying the show. "Won't your neighbors wonder what you're doing with a strange woman in a robe?"

"Ah, but no one can see into my backyard. Didn't you notice? That's the point of pride in this house—total privacy."

"Hmm. Should I worry?"

"I don't know, should you? We could invite the neighbors in if you'd feel safer."

"Do you think they'd bring some ice cream?"

"Oh, blast!" he yelled. "Get it out of the bag and put it in the freezer, would you? I forgot it was there. It's probably soup by now."

Anne found it buried at the bottom of the bag, wrapped in a freezer bag and hard as a rock. "Oh, Stephen! Pralines and cream! On second thought, don't ask anyone over! I want it all."

As she put the ice cream in the freezer, Stephen kept working with the wine bottle. "Also, there's a big quilt in the garage that I use for picnics. It's just on the other side of the door—you'll see a shelf up to your right. Why don't you lay it outside so it'll air out a little. We can eat on that...." His voice trailed off. "I'll get this thing open if it's...the last thing I do." He sure looked sexy with his teeth clenched.

Anne smiled to herself as she headed for the door. So what was a little cork. It would sink to the bottom of the glass, anyway. But then she shuddered. Getting a piece of cork in her mouth always made her think of those little worms floating around in Mexican tequila bottles.

In the two hours that passed between preparations and the shared task of dinner dishes, night settled in and the mood became serene and mellow. Stephen poured a light mint liqueur over ice, and they returned outside to enjoy it on the patio.

Stepping through the doorway, Anne felt the light canyon breeze as it lazily played soft music on the delicate glass chimes. The heat of the day still emanated its warmth, and the sharp, sweet scent of night-blooming jasmine had just begun to linger in the evening air. With the house lights dimmed, there was only soft moonlight casting a silvery shimmer over the lawn. A little paradise all their own.

As Anne carried her glass to the overstuffed sofa, her glance fell on Stephen's cat. Onassis had fallen fast asleep, his white, furry tummy carelessly exposed.

Setting their glasses on the table, Stephen lowered himself onto the sofa, pulling Anne down next to him so that she was curled up across his lap, her head cradled in the crook of his arm.

"My own little bundle of joy," he teased. Even in the moonlight she could see the playful twinkle in his warm, brown eyes.

Anne slipped her arm around his neck, brushing the back of his hair with her hand. She felt safe from the world as she looked contentedly at him. "You know, I've never felt this way with anyone in my life," she whispered. "I can't even remember what it was like not to have you in my life."

"Do you want to remember?"

"No." She touched the corner of Stephen's mouth with her finger, tracing the line of his lips. "Perfect," she murmured, entranced by its masculine curve. Anne felt an almost imperceptible tension creep into his body, but she didn't stop.

After a moment Stephen's eyes dropped to her lips, watching her hint of a smile as she sensed his growing arousal. "Careful," he said, his voice low.

But Anne kept it up, meeting his eyes tauntingly as she became intrigued by the growing feeling of suspense she was creating. Stephen squinted slightly, appraising her actions. Then ever so slowly, a smile appeared at the corners of his mouth. She had answered his silent question.

He took her hand in his and softly kissed her knuckles. Then slowly he led her hand to his throat and teasingly moved it downward, watching her reaction.

"You take my breath away," Anne said, lost in the feeling of his naked chest against her hand. Raising the arm that cradled her head, pulling her closer, Stephen gave her a long, lingering kiss.

Anne closed her eyes, feeling her whole body weaken as his tongue passed across her lips and then retreated. Then she felt it again, slowly licking her lips in a symbolic, primitive suggestion.

Seemingly intent on driving her mad, Stephen slowly broke from her kiss and slid his mouth over the tendon between her neck and her shoulder, biting her gently as his teeth sent waves of desire through her body.

Anne felt that internal melting sensation that had nearly made her wild on the boat. "Stephen . . ." It was almost a cry.

He gathered her up in his arms and, lifting her effortlessly, carried her to the blanket. All in the same motion, he set her down and covered her body with his, kissing her as though he couldn't get enough of her. After a few moments he moaned softly and rolled over to his back, carrying her with him as he guided her arms around his neck.

Trailing his hands from her elbows past her shoulders, Stephen let his thumbs slide under her arms, but not quite over her breasts. Then they traveled down her sides, feeling the curves of her body as they narrowed to her waist and then rounded into hips.

Anne held her breath as he continued inward, gently pressing his fingers just inside her hipbones. His hands lingered there, tempting her with suspended movement that brought a low moan from her throat.

Stephen pulled slightly away from her kiss; there would soon be no turning back. "Do you want me to stop?"

"No," Anne whispered, feeling more love for this man than she'd ever imagined possible.

"Good," he said, shedding the last ounce of inhibition. Reaching gently between them, he pulled the belted tie from her robe, slowly sliding away the thin cotton fabric along with it. She felt the snaps of his shirt open underneath her, and every inch of her skin became sensitized in anticipation of the soft, thick hair of his chest against her body.

With a low moan Stephen wrapped his arms around her, his hands sliding possessively over her bare back until she moved involuntarily, like a stretching cat under his touch.

He took a long, deep breath. "Good," he repeated softly. He gently rolled her under him again, raising up slightly as he removed the rest of their clothes. Not wanting to alter the suspense of his hands brushing against her, Anne kept her eyes closed, and in the next moment Stephen slowly lowered himself, enticing her.

She opened her eyes almost pleadingly, and she realized he'd been watching her.

"You're beautiful," he said huskily.

"So are you," she whispered, her glance dropping to his magnificent chest before lifting back to his eyes.

A silent communication passed between them as their bodies found each other, and without words she assured him of the trust she felt.

Stephen paused for one last second to relish the moment before abandoning himself to what would dominate all his senses. "Anne, I love you," he whispered, his voice deep with feeling.

"And I love you." It was like exchanging a solemn vow, and then those ancient three words of commitment, repeated over and over again, became lost under Stephen's kiss.

Delicately tasting at first, he gradually carried a moment of exquisite tenderness into a world of vivid sensation, and from there, into a flood of emotion. Anne felt herself being swept along. From far away she heard her own voice, but she didn't know what she was saying.

"Oh, God," Stephen whispered, his eyes closing. His mouth hungrily covered hers once more, no longer with the restraint that had been there before. His kiss was possessively forceful yet sweet, on her mouth, her neck, her shoulders, sending shivers through her being. He said her name over and over again, and she responded to his growing intensity as though they were of a single mind.

Stephen's love mounted to a rugged passion that trapped her equally between torment and release. But suddenly he hesitated, and every fiber in her body seemed to quiver with suspended tension.

Anne opened her eyes to search his, and she found them tightly closed as he bit his lower lip to savor the moment for one last second. Then his eyebrows drew together ever so slowly, and she watched for a time-frozen moment as every feature, every slight change in Stephen's expression mirrored the final surrender to a force so powerful that it carried her along to her own resolution. Anne lost herself in the sensation of her whole being seeming to melt in unity with his. It was as though they'd become liquefied together, body and soul, then solidified into one.

After a long while Stephen nuzzled into her neck as his kisses softly beckoned her to join him in the bittersweet aftermath of ultimate possession.

"Stephen—" she whispered. "Oh, Stephen . . ." She started to cry, tears of tender emotion overwhelming her as he hugged her protectively under him.

"I love you, Anne. I'll never stop loving you." And he kissed her tears away.

10

THE NIGHT AIR had still been warm during Anne's late drive home, but typical of Southern California summers, it turned crisp in the early hours of the morning. Anne pulled her time-worn down comforter up around her neck, rolling into it like a cocoon. Just awake enough for her mind to drift, she wanted to stay suspended between realities: her moments with Stephen only hours before and an otherwise normal workday, only hours ahead.

Her thoughts slipped to Stephen and their being together on the blanket. *Lord*, she thought, *I didn't know anything could be so . . .*

No word came to mind to describe what they had shared, the heights of emotion. Anne shivered at the recollection of Stephen's face, reflecting every sensation. Not a bone of in-hibition interfered with that man's pleasures.

Nor hers, Anne reminded herself, still amazed at the way she'd responded. Such passion had been described in books, but she'd never imagined really feeling like that. Not in a million years.

Smiling contentedly, she finally opened one eye. The sun was just starting to peek through her window, and its steady progress announced another bursting summer day.

Anne stretched long and hard, groaning as she tightened every muscle in her body. Then, collapsing them all at once, she laughed. "'What made Marge burn the toast and miss her favorite soap opera?'"

"Sex!" she shouted, throwing back the feather-stuffed German plummel. Then, drawing her legs to her chest, she bounced out of bed.

Ten minutes later, jarred fully awake by the splash of cold water on her face, Anne went into the living room to turn on the televised aerobics program. Now more than ever she wanted to stay in shape.

Starting the movements slowly at first, she let her mind wander to the office and how at home she'd begun to feel at K&W. Especially with Tomlin there.

That dear man. Something about him made Anne realize how sorely she'd missed having a father. And she could just feel the trust he was beginning to have in her. It showed in everything he did.

Suddenly everything seemed so perfect! Stephen, the office, just everything.

Anne hopped through the commercial, not wanting to break the aerobic rhythm she was attaining. She watched as the two babies wet on their diapers, and knowing already which one wouldn't leak through onto the towel, she made several circles around the living room as her thoughts roamed where they would.

The monthly partners' meeting was here again, and Tomlin was actually going to present her ideas for turning the firm into a full-fledged adult. Anne couldn't help but smile to herself. At first he'd challenged her reasoning on every single point, but she'd won him over on each question until he'd just started deferring to her personnel philosophies with less and less inquiry.

That was good. She wanted to make as many independent marks on the firm as she could—while she could. Then if Trudy did stay in Oregon as planned, the way things were now looking Anne just might have the track record she needed to override any outside competition, hands down.

And with Tomlin on her side? Well, that added bit of support was even more than she'd hoped for.

The commercial was over, but she knew the routine so well that her movements came without requiring much attention.

Anne continued to ponder her progress at K&W, but within a moment that persistent, churning sensation was tugging at her stomach again, only this time she couldn't ignore it. Before the question had only been whether Trudy would return. But now, assuming that Trudy did stay in Oregon, what about Stephen?

Anne had consciously avoided thinking about that growing conflict, but last night had brought a reality that couldn't be pushed off any longer. Any way she tried to slice it, she was in love, and falling in love with one of K&W's partners certainly wasn't a complication she'd taken into account when deciding to leave a job she couldn't replace.

Suddenly she wanted to tell Stephen everything, just blurt it all out and hope for his support. But Anne had to acknowledge the deep fear she'd been hiding. At this early stage her one-way, nonrefundable ticket into K&W could drive him away.

Oh, why worry prematurely, she silently argued. *Maybe once everything settles into a pattern, Stephen will just get used to the secrecy. Then as time goes on, maybe he'll even feel different about it.* But somehow that seemed too hard to imagine.

Uncomfortable with the turn her thoughts had taken, Anne willed her eyes back to the aerobics program. She riveted her attention on it as though seeing it for the very first time.

As the workout drew to its gradual close, Anne pressed her sleeve on her forehead for a long moment while she caught her breath. Then, returning to the bathroom, she filled her mind with nothing more complex than the recollection of how good that cold shower had felt at Stephen's.

Setting the water to the same cool temperature, Anne climbed into the tub. She stood there for a long moment, letting all thoughts give way to sensation as the steady beads streamed over her head and down her body. If only she didn't have a brain, she finally concluded. Then life would be so simple. No logic, no plans, no worries about careers. Just sensations. One after another. Like last night....

With a little grin Anne reached for the shampoo. Strange, she thought, looking at it critically. Her bottle of the same brand didn't arouse any of the fond emotion that Stephen's had.

TRAFFIC WAS LIGHT at that early hour. It was only seven twenty-five when Anne snapped on the lights in the office reception room. Five more minutes found her immersed in the papers on her desk, and except for Stephen's creeping into her mind at the oddest moments, she was able to enjoy the bliss of deep concentration with no one there to interrupt.

But as people started arriving, Anne began feeling twinges of nervousness. Encountering Stephen in the office would seem so out of place after the intimate evening they'd shared in the privacy of his house. Anne wasn't quite sure how to act under such circumstances, yet she had an intuitive sense that their first contact would have to put him totally at ease. She didn't have to wait long to see if she could do it.

"Anne Michaels," she answered, silencing the first ring of her telephone. It was nine-twenty.

"Good morning," said Tomlin. "What kind of shape is your cost analysis in?" There was the slightest edge to his voice.

"I have it in my typewriter right now," she replied. "I'm almost finished, but I wanted to summarize the benefits in categories so the partners can—"

"Bring in what you have, will you?" He hung up.

That's interesting, Anne thought, replacing the receiver with a curious frown. She pulled the short tail-end section she'd been working on and brought the whole proposal into Tomlin's office.

Instead of being greeted by Tomlin alone, she encountered two unexpected guests—Mr. Cooper and Stephen. Anne was taken totally by surprise, but she managed not to signal any particular recognition.

"I was just chatting with Merrifield and Cooper," began Tomlin. "I've been telling them about some of your ideas, and Mr. Cooper was curious to see what you were coming up with."

There was a slight note of tension in the air, and Anne caught herself from looking at Stephen for a clue. "Certainly," she said, handing Mr. Cooper her report.

The trio looked as though they'd been in conference for some time. Stephen was sprawled on the couch, and Mr. Cooper sat in one of the two chairs across from Tomlin, very much owning his space. He didn't look receptive at all, and as he began reading the proposal Tomlin motioned for Anne to take the remaining chair across from his desk. Unfortunately it faced Stephen's side of the room, with Cooper in between.

Anne avoided Stephen's eyes while the four of them sat there in silence, the only sound being an occasional rustle of paper as Mr. Cooper turned a page. She couldn't read the expression on Tomlin's face, but she sensed he'd come up against some resistance.

As though to pass the time, he began making a note to himself, and Anne finally ventured a guarded glance at Stephen. He looked as if he'd been watching her, and she thought she perceived just the slightest attempt at communication on his face when they made eye contact. If Tomlin just raised his eyes, he could see either of them, so Anne gave Stephen the same polite smile she'd have given anyone. Then she lowered her gaze to the rich patina of Tomlin's desk.

After a moment Mr. Cooper cleared his throat and took off his glasses, laying them on the desk with measured slowness. "That's quite a proposition," he said. In typical lawyer form he'd conveyed nothing, and the silence he was leaving said he didn't plan on adding anything to it.

"Do you like it, or do you hate it?" Anne asked. She felt nervous, but she was amazed at how controlled she sounded.

"Neither," he said. "I'm wondering, however, why it would be necessary to add what appears to be a substantial increase in overhead when we haven't been receiving any complaints from the staff."

Anne looked at Tomlin, but he was going to let her handle it on her own.

"Well, Mr. Tomlin wanted to see how we measured up with other firms our size, and as I got into the major causes for turnover in larger offices, that's what I came up with—lack of clearly defined policies and poor benefits."

"I see," said Mr. Cooper. "How is it that we've been able to keep our employees happy in the past, then?" He was still looking at her expressionlessly.

Anne kept her voice tactfully polite. "Because until recently you've been two small firms, Mr. Cooper. All the employees are originals."

"I see," he said, stroking his chin pensively. "And you think we need to suddenly start monitoring the staff with unaccustomed structure and offering benefits that would delight any union?"

Anne hesitated. "No, but I do think the original policies need to be altered to accommodate K&W's increased size in order to absorb turnover without chaos."

Mr. Cooper leaned forward in his seat and took a sip of his coffee before looking at her dead in the eyes. Anne had heard about this side of him. He used silences to make you squirm and blither, so she did neither.

"I understand my secretary wasn't pleased with the idea of the sign-in sheet. Were you aware of that?"

Anne had wondered when he'd get to that point. "Yes. Jean made that very clear."

"How have you . . . handled it?"

She felt a smile cross her face that was slightly shy yet in no way apologetic. "I've ignored it," she said.

Cooper laughed abruptly. "So have I. Up until now, anyway. She's asked me to exempt her from the sign-in procedures."

Anne shook her head. "She said she was going to, and that's why I've ignored it. I haven't heard from you either way."

"She does run a lot of errands for me, you know."

"That's true." Anne nodded. "But once again, what if there were a fire on the floor and there was no way of knowing whether she was out on one of your errands or caught in the Xerox room? K&W is no longer small enough for a quick nose count to be taken in an emergency, and with a sign-in sheet there aren't any questions."

Mr. Cooper raised his eyebrows, leaving a long silence. "Interesting point," he finally said, then cleared his throat. Had his wall lowered? Maybe an inch?

Hoping to get off the defensive, Anne took advantage of the moment. "Mr. Cooper, if I could address the proposal in the vaguest generalities, I think its logic would seem more reasonable. Especially when you see a cost analysis over the long term," she added.

After a moment's hesitation, he merely nodded. But for the next twenty minutes, in spite of himself, Mr. Cooper lis-

tened to Anne with a look of increasing interest on his face
as she dredged up horror stories about other firms that had
eventually fragmented over mismanagement in their early
stages. With the legal community comprising such a small
world, he knew them all, and Anne used specific examples
so that there could be no question about the inside knowledge she'd acquired, as well, or about the conservative approach she'd actually taken.

When she'd finished a moment of pensive silence went by,
and Anne did nothing to fill it. Finally Mr. Cooper took a
deep breath and turned his glance on Mr. Tomlin. "I'm beginning to see what you mean, Harold."

Anne immediately looked to Tomlin for a clue, but his face
was innocently unexpressive. "Thank you, my dear," he said
simply. "Could you make a copy of this for us?" His cryptic
smile was equally unreadable.

Anne got up to leave. "Do you mind if I finish it first?"

Mr. Cooper's eyebrows raised incredulously. "You
mean . . . there's *more*?"

Anne's glance darted to Stephen for a split second, and she
saw a suppressed grin at the corners of his mouth. But there
was also unguarded affection in his eyes.

Afraid of blushing, she quickly pulled her gaze back to the
report. "Just little things," she said. "A few general para-
graphs about possible low-cost incentive options—morale
builders and things like that."

Cooper hesitantly handed over the report, and as Anne
walked toward the door she shot a glance at Stephen. He'd
barely moved during the discussion, but something told her
he'd found the whole thing quite amusing. "Mr. Merrifield,"
she said as she passed him.

"*Whew.*" Anne whistled as she closed her office door. Mr.
Cooper could be a frightening little devil when he wanted. No

wonder Jean was so tetchy. The woman must have nerves o
steel.

Dropping the proposal on her desk, Anne decided to run
downstairs to get a Danish to go. Maybe something in her
stomach would have a calming effect, because at the mo
ment she felt she'd been put through a ringer.

She was just sipping the last of the milk when the phone
rang. "Anne Michaels," she answered between swallows.

"You were great," Stephen said quietly.

"Oh, Stephen! What in the world was the man doing?"

"Fixing to make you look like an idiot. He and Tomlin had
gotten into a little argument over the necessity of increasing
regulations 'and/or' overhead—with great emphasis on the
latter, I might add. Cooper couldn't understand why things
shouldn't just stay as they were, particularly since he and
Tomlin had agreed on it just two months ago. But since
you've been here? Ah, Tomlin's become a turncoat!" Ste
phen chuckled as though he'd been watching two children
deeply involved in a game of war.

"But the man can be terrifying!"

Stephen erupted into a laugh of irony. "Why, that's ex
actly what he said about you!"

"Now I don't believe that for one minute." She laughed a
the thought.

"Nope. You pulled the rug right out from under him. Me
too, for that matter. Cooper likes to make mincemeat out o
people from time to time, and I thought you handled it quite
well."

"I just responded honestly."

"But you don't understand. He's used to having people fal
all over themselves when he gets his 'justify your existence
tactics going. You just kept giving him these simple answer:
he couldn't argue with. That's an impressive tack when you're
supposed to be floundering."

Anne lowered her voice. "I thought *we* did rather well in the same room together, didn't you?"

"You, for sure, get an A. I hadn't intended to be in on any of that, but they'd locked horns when I arrived, and I was to be the 'mediating third party.'"

"Well, it does make sense, don't you think?"

"Sweet one, don't ask me. I keep my nose out of administrative things. All I want to do is practice law—" Stephen lowered his voice "—and make love to you."

Suddenly Anne's mind conjured up the vision of Stephen's face in the moonlight, and a soft smile played at her lips. "Do you have any idea in the world how . . . how beautiful you are?"

"Dammit, woman. You took the words right out of my mouth!" Then Stephen paused a moment. "Anne, I love you. I *really* love you." He said it as if it were a matter of great amazement to him.

"Aw, come on," she teased, "you just like my salads."

"That, too. Would you like to go to Ventura this evening? We could go to dinner and a show?"

"In Ventura?"

"Well, it's a nice enough drive, and it sure beats running into someone I know. We can take a walk around the marina if we decide not to go to a movie."

"Okay, you're on. Can I drive your car?"

"Hmm. I can think of much better things for you to occupy yourself with."

Anne laughed, afraid to ask. "Come on, I've never driven a Lincoln before."

"You'll never go back to a Toyota—I'll give you fair warning."

"It's a Nissan."

Stephen's other line rang. "See you tonight."

"Oh! Where?"

"Meet me at the end of Wilshire. There's a parking lot near there where we can leave your car at—" His phone kept ringing. "I'll call you before I leave." He clicked off.

Anne finished her report and Xeroxed it over the noon hour. She looked it over to be sure it was all there before bringing it to Tomlin. He seldom went to lunch at noon, and she was curious to know what he'd say about the morning's encounter.

"Hello, my dear, come on in!" He was standing at the credenza looking for a file.

Mable was out to lunch, but Anne shut the door out of habit before crossing his office with the report.

"Anne, you're a delight." He chortled. "Cooper should stay out of personnel. He hates dealing with it and has no feeling for it besides. Why, anyone can see that it makes perfect sense to take remedial action prior to having a mess on your hands."

Tomlin had a short memory, Anne mused. "Did Cooper see that 'perfect sense'?"

"I don't know, but I do think he's going to advise that secretary of his that she'll have to start signing in. You might like to know, incidentally, that I've had several of the attorneys mention to me that their secretaries have kept better hours since that thing's been sitting at the front desk."

"I'm glad to hear that. There wasn't as much resistance to it as I thought there'd be."

Tomlin smiled. "I suspect word got out that the firm was thinking about considering increased benefits, as well?"

"Now I didn't say a thing that would commit anyone to anything," Anne defended.

"I know." He laughed. "Mable heard some of our discussion, and I think she said something. It doesn't matter." He found the file he'd been looking for and tucked it under his arm to take it somewhere.

Anne looked down at her report. "Mr. Tomlin, I want you to know something. I really appreciate the way you've . . ." She hadn't intended to say anything to him, and she didn't know where she was going with it.

Tomlin saw her hesitation, and he smiled, putting his arm around her as they slowly crossed the Persian rug. "I'm afraid the firm doesn't look too kindly on inner-office romances, my dear," he said sadly, opening the door for her.

Anne's heart jumped into her throat.

"Otherwise," he continued, "I'd divorce that battle-ax I'm married to and propose!"

"Oh, help!" Anne gasped, breaking into laughter. If anything, Mrs. Tomlin was known for her lovely disposition and ladylike demeanor.

"Only kidding," Tomlin teased as they passed Mable's desk and started down the hall. "I don't know what I'd do without her. Mary has always wanted a daughter, you know. I always thought they'd be more trouble than they'd be worth, but who knows? Maybe she was right." His smile faded into an expression of melancholy.

As Tomlin continued down the hall alone, Anne returned to her office and closed the door, not quite understanding the silly lump in her throat.

11

OVER THE NEXT MONTH life settled into a pattern that for Anne and Stephen was anything but normal. Stephen seemed to be silently counting the days until their relationship could "come out of the closet," as he put it, and Anne did her best to avoid the subject entirely.

Fighting twinges of guilt over a valid fear that could have the appearance of deceit, Anne more than once came within an inch of laying her cards on the table. But every time she panicked. After all, there were really no cards in her hand, only a stack of "ifs." In two or three months, though? Anything could happen. She saw no choice but to wait.

But as far as their relationship could go in that time, it went beautifully. Anne Michaels and Stephen Merrifield were in love, as much as any two people could be in love. They spent most of their evenings safely hidden away in the privacy of Stephen's house, and it soon became a natural part of their lives to be together in a home setting.

Yet as quiet and serene as the evenings were, Anne's days were the busiest and most exciting she'd ever spent. The partners had approved her final proposal for benefits and policy changes, and she'd been given the authority to institute them all.

Two delicately balanced worlds, each perfect. Each kept separate.

One morning as Anne was wrapping up final negotiations with the new insurance company, Tomlin called her into his office. "Close the door," he said, looking like a cat who'd just discovered a private supply of mouse holes.

"Oh, dear." She sighed, wary of his expression as she crossed the floor to his desk. "What could you possibly be up to, Mr. Tomlin?"

He could hardly contain himself, but he whispered as though they could be heard. "I've just been advised that the whole seventh floor is going to become available!"

Anne stared at him blankly, taking a seat across from him.

"I want you to drop whatever you're doing and begin finding out about subleasing extra offices to sole practitioners." He looked at her with a cagey twinkle in his eyes.

Anne grinned. "But what in the world is so secret—"

Tomlin stopped the rest of her sentence with a wave of his hands. "My partners are giving some foolish thought to relocating our offices to Century City." He rubbed his hands together like an old miser. "I *hate* that place. I want to stay in Beverly Hills, and this is going to be my chance!"

Tomlin leaned across the desk, his eyes flashing with a diabolical plan. "We're outgrowing this suite, you see? And there's just no office space in Beverly Hills, anywhere! Our lease will be up soon, so they think it would be wise to move while there are still choices in that cement jungle of Century City."

"Ah," said Anne, the light slowly dawning as the gleam deepened in Tomlin's eyes.

"'Ah' is right. The brokerage company on the seventh floor has just been bought out, and they're disbanding! It hasn't even been made public yet, but the president is an old client of mine. Not only that, but they want to move at once!"

Tomlin leaned even closer as his expression became wary. "The problem is, we'd have to take the entire floor. I happen to know that there's someone else in the building who'll want it lock, stock and barrel as soon as the word is out, so we'll have to act very quickly. And very quietly," he added.

"But Mr. Tomlin, except for maybe two or three offices, isn't that just about twice the space you need?"

"Of course! That's why I'm telling you all this! Darn it, girl, every now and then you just don't grasp the obvious," he scolded. "That's precisely why I'd like to know the feasibility of taking a whole floor and renting what we don't need now to individual practitioners. Then, as we need it for growth, we'll have it. Office by office. You see?"

"Finally. I'm afraid you move a little fast for me sometimes."

Tomlin looked almost impish as his voice lowered again. "If we had access to another whole floor, then there certainly couldn't be any reason not to renew our lease here on the eighth floor, could there? And by the time we could possibly outgrow all that, I will have disintegrated to mere dust! I'd *never* have to worry about fighting that Century City traffic. That whole place gives me the creeps with its cement. It's all cement!"

Anne's laugh became one of sheer amusement. He could be so dramatic for someone who looked so bland. "Okay," she agreed, "how do I go about it?"

"Quietly," he warned. "Look in the *Daily Journal* and find out how much a fellow pays for an individual office in an existing law suite. Make some calls—with your door closed, of course. See what the problems are in subleasing to a bunch of sole practitioners. Find out about turnover, how difficult it is to find tenants—the works!

"Then go see a few of them and get an idea of what kind of facilities they offer, what's included in the rent and the like. You know, snoop! Just snoop. Women are good at that."

"All right," said Anne, shaking her head affectionately.

"Oh, start this very minute! I don't want to lose even a second!" Tomlin winked conspiratorially as he handed her a copy of the legal trade paper.

A number of calls revealed that subleasing covered everything from a small firm leasing out one spare office to a conglomerate that made a business out of it. Anne made appointments to see several of them around the lunch hour and returned at four o'clock with enough information to give Tomlin everything he needed.

He was delighted. He'd been on the phone all afternoon with the building, negotiating a new lease.

Anne stared at him in awe. "Mr. Tomlin, won't your partners get rather upset that you're arranging all this without even discussing it with them?"

"Have I signed anything?" he asked innocently. But he was barely able to contain his enthusiasm, and his legal pad was filled with telltale calculations.

She rolled her eyes. "Here we go," she sighed. "Let me know if you need anything else."

"Oh, I will, my dear, I will! Thank you. You've done quite well." Then he covered his mouth with his hand, squinching his eyebrows together. "I never thought for a minute we'd be able to get more space in this building!"

Anne left his office with a deep sigh. The more his personality unfolded, the more she wondered how anyone could find him frightening.

THAT NIGHT, boning chicken breasts while Stephen chopped vegetables for the wok, Anne was considering Tomlin's plan when she caught sight of an envelope next to the phone. It had a Boston address in the upper left-hand corner.

Except for Trudy's return, the only other topic that ever seemed to be avoided was Stephen's ex-wife, and there was always a foreboding darkness about Stephen's expression whenever her name came up. Anne had made a point of keeping her questions to herself, but with that piece of mail lying there in plain sight, it seemed a good time to venture.

"What ever happened to Cathy's idea for a children's ballet school?"

"She's opened it," said Stephen, motioning toward the stack of mail. "I got a letter from her, and she's already signed a lease for a studio." For once he seemed relatively relaxed about the subject.

Anne recalled the photograph she'd found. "Was she a professional dancer herself at one time?"

Stephen paused before he answered. "Yes, she was a professional dancer herself." But there was an unmistakable hint of tension in his voice, and Anne treaded lightly, keeping the topic restricted to the school.

"I would think that would be such fun," she pondered innocently. "Teaching little girls to dance. Knowing that some day one of them may become a prima ballerina, and you've been the one to—"

Stephen's involuntary wince interrupted her sentence. He immediately checked it, but he couldn't quite hide the strain in his voice. "If training someone else to be a prima ballerina is something you've always longed to do, then it probably would be fun. Do you want me to use these?"

Anne's eyes fell from Stephen's closed expression to the week-old bag of mushrooms he was holding. They'd clearly seen their last day, and considering his almost comical obsession about freshness, the question made a statement of its own.

Forcing a casual expression, Anne shook her head nonchalantly as she pushed the new box across the counter with the back of a greasy hand. Whatever the sore spot was regarding Cathy, it seemed to center more on her dancing than on her personally.

Looking for another subject, Anne took only a moment to find one that made her smile. Stephen shared Tomlin's dread of Century City, and Anne knew it would be safe to tell him about the secret plan.

Stephen laughed as she began describing how deviously Tomlin was gathering ammunition, but there was just a hint of something in his expression that looked like concern. Probably just a carryover from talking about Cathy, Anne surmised, and she continued her story about how she and Tomlin were quietly investigating the possibilities.

But the look of concern in Stephen's face persisted. "You and Tomlin are getting rather tight, aren't you?"

Now it was Anne's turn at avoidance. "Well, I have to admit, Stephen, I've been thinking of dropping you and marrying him as soon as I've had my fill of your warm, sweet body." She leaned across the chopping island and winked. "But don't worry, baby, we can still be lovers."

Stephen frowned, ignoring the joke. "That wasn't what I meant. It just seems you're . . . entrenching, that's all."

This was fast becoming one of those occasions when Anne wanted to address the point head-on, but she knew it wasn't the time. Besides, there was nothing to address—yet.

Taking a left turn into a side subject, Anne centered on something that was very much the truth. "I guess I am developing quite an affection for him, Stephen. I've never had a father, and Tomlin is about as fatherly a soul as I've ever met."

Anne held the half-boned breast of chicken in the air as she continued, her mind conjuring up a picture of Tomlin at his desk. "He's just so . . . so darling! I mean, the way he schemes and plans. Why, you can just see the wheels turning!" She shook her head fondly as she returned to the task of prying meat off the bone.

Stephen's expression relaxed, and seeming to shed his concern, he resumed his diagonal slicing. He had it down to a science.

After a moment an affectionate grin began twitching the corners of his mouth. "You're right," he admitted. "I can just see him. Hiding in his office, getting every little detail worked out in advance. . . ." Stephen laughed finally, arching an eyebrow in admiration.

"Oh, that's precisely what he's doing. I'll bet he's going to spend the whole evening looking for a round of bullets to put in the chamber, just in case someone comes on an argument he hadn't thought of."

Stephen gave her a mock warning glance. "Well, knowing Tomlin as I do, he'll have three more rounds tucked away in his breast pocket." He grinned as he reached for the pile of Italian squashes. "Just wait. Tomorrow morning he'll have all the partners in there, and he'll have an airtight argument for every possible reason for not staying in the building. By the time he's through, anyone disagreeing will look like a blithering idiot."

Anne wiped her hands on a paper towel. "Well, just from what I saw today, it would be better financially to stay. I stopped down on the seventh floor, and a good half of it wouldn't need more than a touch of remodeling. Considering the layouts of some of the rental suites I saw, the other half wouldn't require much tearing down, either." She grabbed another breast. "Plus he sounded like he was making a very reasonable deal on the lease."

Stephen's hands stopped their rhythmical motion as he stared at her in amazement. "He was negotiating a lease?"

Anne laughed understandingly, and once more a chicken breast got suspended in midair. "'I haven't *signed* anything, have I?'"

Stephen grinned at the all-too-accurate portrayal. "Well, then, tomorrow the fur really will fly," he predicted, slicing the last of the zucchini.

Scooping the pieces into the designated bowl, Stephen put his knife on the towel and walked over to Anne's side of the counter. Standing behind her, he slid his hands slowly around her waist and nuzzled the back of her neck.

Anne almost reached up to press her hand against his cheek, but catching herself, she held out her gooey fingers. "Sorry."

"Think nothing of it," said Stephen casually as he unzipped her jeans in one single, efficient pull.

Anne gasped. "Stephen!" Then she started to laugh helplessly. He always caught her off guard with his impulses. He just acted without warning—sometimes without even thinking. Then he winged it from there.

Stephen's low, sensuous laugh sent a shiver down her spine. "Unless you want to get grease all over your nice, clean clothes, you can't really do too much at the moment, now can you?"

Anne looked at her slimy hands as Stephen's quiet, sexy FM disc jockey voice continued talking in her ear. "On the other hand, I could lick them off for you." The index finger of one hand trailed a line of temptation down her spine.

Anne felt her whole body turn to jelly and, holding her head to the side, she looked up into his eyes. "Hmm, now that would be the waste of a clearly marvelous resource." She mimicked the phrase, still remembering it from the first day they'd met.

Stephen hesitated just a moment. "Okay," he said simply. He sat down on the floor, holding up his hand to take hers.

"Oh, come on." Anne laughed. "You've got to be kidding." She pushed the faucet lever with a dry wrist and began washing her hands as she shook her head in amusement.

"Would I kid about a thing like that?" He remained there.

Onassis saw his opportunity and jumped on Stephen's lap, purring in anticipation of a good back scratch. But a big hand pushed him off just roughly enough for him to get the idea and, as he sauntered away, insulted, Stephen looked back at Anne. There was such determination in his eyes.

"Oh, Stephen, come on. We can't," she pleaded, laughing as she dried her hands.

But all she got for an answer was a reassuring wink.

"Right . . . *here*?"

"Right here," he confirmed. Stephen reached up and turned off the noodles. Then, catching her hand, he gently pulled her down with him.

"But you'll mess up my hair," Anne teased.

"I'm sure I will," he said. Gently pressing her back against the soft rug, Stephen licked the tendon between her neck and shoulder and then slowly slid his teeth over it.

A shiver seemed to come from somewhere deep inside Anne's body. "But what about dinner?" Her voice had become a whisper.

"I'll have you instead."

Anne laughed. "But what about me—I'm starving."

Stephen pulled away just for a second, and his eyes dropped to her mouth. He said nothing, but a little smile played at the corners of his eyes before he gave her a long, slow kiss. Then he began licking her lips in that sensuous way he had.

"Mmm," she encouraged, still not quite over the fact that she was rapidly getting as uninhibited as he was. But as Stephen's gentle bites moved from her throat down past the hollow of her collarbone, that was Anne's last rational thought.

STEPHEN HAD BEEN RIGHT, mused Anne when she arrived at the office the following morning. All the partners were in Tomlin's office with the door closed.

Several of the secretaries stopped by to ask if she knew what was happening, but she shook her head. "I don't know anything for sure," she said, "but I'm using their unified absence to catch up on my filing."

At eleven o'clock Tomlin's door finally opened, and the partners quietly came out. Dying to know what had happened, Anne stayed by her phone. She saw Stephen walk down the hall on his way to his office, but his expression told her nothing. He gave her an almost-imperceptible wink just as he passed, but she didn't know whether that related to the outcome of the meeting, or to the kitchen floor.

When Mr. Cooper went by, Anne figured he'd have been the last to linger, so she took a casual stroll by Tomlin's office. He was inside alone, and Mable was away from her desk.

Anne stuck her head through the door. "Good morning," she called, her voice singing a question.

"Good morning!" He looked triumphant.

She yawned long and dramatically, feigning boredom. "When?" she asked.

Tomlin was trying to suppress his delight, but a devilish grin gave him away. "It's not certain yet. It depends on how long a lease we can get. They're going to get back to me, but it looks extremely good." He sat back in his chair.

"You don't lose, do you?" Anne teased, shaking her head.

"I try not to, but sometimes I do," he said, calling on his most modest expression. But it was wasted on Anne.

"Just for form, though, right?"

The hint of a guilty smile broke through. "You're beginning to venture opinions on matters you know nothing about, my dear."

She tilted her head. "Hmm, maybe, Mr. Tomlin—" But suddenly her eye was caught by the slowest wink she'd ever seen.

ANNE WAS LIKE A FLY on the wall for the next few days as she watched Tomlin get his way. There was excitement in the air, with meetings and negotiations taking place in his office, the building office and on the seventh floor itself.

The brokerage firm wanted to move as quickly as possible, and they were hoping for somewhere between thirty and sixty days. Little did they know what luck they were in. With Tomlin's compulsion to get a thing into his pocket and sewn up, he pushed for taking over the suite immediately.

There were more meetings to decide how the space was going to be used, and the final outcome was that the whole litigation department was going to move onto the seventh floor.

Anne was ecstatic about the news. Certainly with Stephen on a different floor entirely, that would solve the bulk of his problem! Sure she still worked for his firm, but they wouldn't run into each other in the halls anymore, and except for the times she had to be in the litigation department, they might not even see each other at all. Litigation almost operated like a separate entity, anyway. This had to be a gift from heaven.

Somehow Anne managed to contain her excitement around Stephen. She didn't want to open any cans of worms prematurely, before he actually had a chance to see for himself that things could be worked out. But once he saw how easy it could be, surely he'd soften his position. Of course!

The more Anne thought about it, the more convinced she became that this single stroke was the break she'd been waiting for. If Trudy did come back, maybe Anne could stay on in some assistant capacity, since there would be the added responsibility of acting as a leasing agent. And if Trudy de-

:ided not to return, by then Anne would have seen the firm
through a move that could be heavily disruptive or not, depending on the person in charge. Assuming she handled that
well, what reason would K&W possibly have for not making her a permanent offer?

Then, after she'd had a whole year of subleasing responsibility on top of the usual management functions, her abil-
ities would finally be obvious. Anne Michaels would be in a
whole different league. She could take that experience anywhere!

Now all that remained was for her to keep doing as good
a job as she could. She crossed her fingers and cleared her
desk. There was work to do!

Anne spent hours on the phone with the telephone company, meticulously making sure they understood exactly
what was needed. She screened space planners, painting
companies, carpet people and interior designers. As soon as
she found someone who sounded competent and easy to deal
with, she passed the person on to Tomlin.

Whatever he was doing, he'd interrupt it. Little did he
know that for once his compulsion to expedite things was
exceeded by Anne's. She had never been so busy or so happy
in her entire life.

Until one afternoon. One little phone call turned the tide.

12

"ANNE MICHAELS," she answered brightly.

There was a slight pause. "Anne, would you come into my office?" Tomlin's voice sounded different.

"Sure. Is anything wrong?"

"I just talked to Trudy," he said.

Anne went numb. "I'll be right in."

She walked like an automaton into Tomlin's office and closed the door behind her. He was sitting at his desk with a serious look on his face. "Trudy has just informed me that she's planning to stay in Oregon."

Anne stared at him, not believing what she'd heard. Trudy couldn't do that to her. It had only been four months. Now more than ever, with Stephen in the picture, she desperately needed the other two months to prove her worth.

Tomlin cleared his throat. "It came as quite a surprise to me, but I believe she's made up her mind."

"Did . . . did she call you?"

"No. I called her. I suspected something was wrong when so much time went by without hearing from her, so I wanted to see how she was doing. She sounded somewhat stilted in our conversation, and I asked her how it felt to be home. Then, as she elaborated upon the merits of Oregon, she didn't sound like someone who was planning to leave again, so I asked. Trudy never was very good at hiding feelings of exuberance," he added.

Anne was dumbfounded. "Is it certain?" She didn't know what else to say.

"I think so," he said, looking at her gravely.

"Well," Anne said conclusively, looking down at the chains on her right wrist. "So where do we go from here?" Her voice sounded strained to her own ears.

Tomlin took a deep breath. "I don't know. Needless to say, I'm going to have to give the matter some thought. The timing couldn't be worse, considering everything else."

He sighed, looking suddenly tired. "Those of my partners who were the losing proponents of Century City have also gone on record as wanting to conduct a search for a professional management specialist—even before Trudy's departure."

"I see," said Anne. *But I can do it!* she thought.

"I'll have to discuss it with them and see just how we can pursue the best solution."

"Of course," Anne said, but her voice was flat.

Tomlin sat across from her with a soft look in his eyes, but she couldn't read it. After a moment he spoke. "In the meantime, shall we just continue along? There needn't be any rush, and certainly in view of this change, you'd be given considerable notice before any decision would be made."

"All right." Anne was in too much shock to offer anything other than bland agreement.

Tomlin seemed to consider adding something to what he'd said, but then his eyes lowered. That wasn't a good sign.

"All right," she repeated, rising to leave.

Anne was like a zombie the rest of the day, impervious to all that went on around her yet somehow managing to function. She and Stephen talked only briefly on the phone in the late afternoon, and he said he had to be in Thousand Oaks for a seven o'clock dinner meeting, but he'd stop at her apartment for a quick cup of coffee on his way. That was fine with Anne. More than anything she needed time to think.

TWO HOURS LATER she heard him bounding up the stairs. He was whistling, and his knock had a merrily urgent sound.

"Well! Good news!" he said, looking as happy as a clam.

"What's the good news?" Anne had trouble suppressing a glare as she stepped aside, passively receiving his brisk peck on the cheek.

"We won't have to sneak around anymore! Trudy just saved us two months! Well, two months less the time it takes the firm to find someone to replace her, that is. Then once you leave, we can date a couple of months for appearances, and then—"

"Yes," she interrupted, "and the bad news is that I'm out of a job!"

Stephen grinned as he followed her into the kitchen. "Well, I don't see what difference that would make if—"

"You don't see what *difference* it would make!" Anne spun around, her eyes brimming. "Stephen, you don't understand!"

His smile slowly faded, and he pulled up a chair. "Well, maybe I don't. Why don't you explain it to me?"

Anne poured two cups of freshly brewed coffee and sat down across from him. She took her head in her hands, thoroughly confused. "Stephen, I'm really heavily invested in this not happening—so soon."

"Is there something I'm missing?" His innocent question made her feel even more hopeless. There was no longer any reason not to tell him all about it, but this wasn't the time. "It's just that I'm right in the middle of everything! I've got the construction people starting in a couple of days, and . . . I'm just not ready for this to happen yet."

"So? They'll find another office manager, and you'll be out of the same job you would have been out of at the end of six months, anyway. So what's the problem? You can go to another firm and manage to your heart's content, if you really feel you must keep working."

Anne was so distraught that she only heard half of what he was saying. "Stephen, at this point I have four months as a temporary office manager, and only three of them consist of anything other than calling for an occasional temp. Now that I'm just starting to get involved in things, Trudy talks to Mr. Tomlin and pulls the rug right out from under me!"

"And you thought with six months you'd be in a better position?"

She fell silent. It was all happening too fast.

"Whew." Stephen whistled. "I thought you'd see it as a blessing."

"I need some time to think, that's all. It just came as rather a surprise."

He thought for a moment and then smiled understandingly. "Maybe you're right. Let's just put the whole thing on hold. You're in no shape to talk about what's for better or for worse tonight." There was a slightly playful twinkle in his eye, but Anne was too upset to remark on it.

Trying to bridge the gap between their two moods, or at least to soften the moment, Stephen began telling her about the client he was meeting. There were some very amusing aspects to the case, and somehow Anne managed to show signs of interest until it was time for him to leave for Thousand Oaks.

But the rest of Anne's evening was filled with one thought and one thought only. She hadn't been at the firm long enough to even hope to be considered for the position herself. If only Trudy had just waited until a month or so after the move! Then not only would Anne have had the additional time she needed, but more important, she knew that Stephen's removal to another floor would have been her only possible way of getting him to see things differently. In one stroke Trudy's premature announcement had ruined the plan on two counts, and Anne needed them both.

She went to bed feeling that the earth had dropped out from under her without notice.

THE NEXT DAY Stephen was in Thousand Oaks again until late afternoon, and Anne was aware of a general hush that seemed to permeate the partners' offices when she was near. Tomlin's door was closed every time she walked by, and she knew various partners had been in for conferences. Probably something to do with the construction, she surmised. Time was drawing near, and there were always last-minute changes.

She continued as best she could to function as though nothing had happened, but the hours passed slowly. As everyone was leaving for the day, Anne wandered by Stephen's office, but his door was closed, as well. It was probably his turn to vote on whatever Tomlin had decided. Knowing he'd call her when he was through, she left.

The phone rang shortly after Anne arrived at the apartment; it was Stephen. His voice sounded unusually stiff. No wonder, she thought, reflecting on the way she'd treated him the previous evening. She forced herself to be as light as possible. "I made a quick stop at the market on my way home. Want to come over for a veggie dinner à la Anne's kitchen?"

Stephen took a breath as though he'd planned to say something else, but he let it seep out through his teeth instead. "Sure. I'll be there shortly." He hung up.

That was abrupt, she thought, frowning to herself. But then he was probably still in the middle of something to do with his new client.

Anne took a quick shower and changed into a pair of jeans and a T-shirt. She'd just started chopping some broccoli when she heard the familiar knock.

Stephen looked at her with a raised eyebrow as he walked into the apartment. "Hi," he said, kissing her on the cheek. "Feeling better tonight?"

"I guess so." She smiled. "It was sort of like a morgue at the office today, and I felt kind of uncomfortable. But the seventh floor breaks ground tomorrow, so to speak, and by ten o'clock I'll be too busy to notice."

Stephen followed her into the kitchen, saying nothing as he poured two glasses of wine. He was a little too quiet.

"Is something wrong?" Her words came out nonchalantly.

There was just a pause as Stephen took a seat at the table. For a moment he just sipped his wine slowly, watching her chopping endeavors with interest. Then he dropped the bomb. "There's been some talk today of making you a permanent job offer."

Anne almost cut herself. "What?"

Stephen's eyes raised to hers, and there was a hint of misgiving in them. "Tomlin's pushing for it. Naturally there's some serious resistance from a few of the partners because you don't have any more background than you do."

Anne was still standing there, frozen. "Stephen . . . *are you serious*?"

"Yes, I am." He continued looking at her appraisingly.

"Why, I never thought—" She was so shocked that she just stood there, speechless.

A dry smile touched Stephen's lips for a moment as he seemed to analyze the glass in his hand. "It's only casual conversation at this point. Tomlin got a call late this afternoon to draft an appeal that's going to eat up every moment of his life over the next week at least, so everything's going on hold, including this Trudy matter."

"Oh, but to think that—" Anne could hardly contain herself. "Tomlin's *pushing* for it?"

"He certainly was today. I'd take it as a compliment."

"Well—" she beamed "—but we all know that whatever Tomlin wants, Tomlin gets!"

Suddenly Anne noticed that Stephen hadn't moved from his position, and he raised his eyes to meet hers. After a long moment he spoke. "Anne, tell me if I'm wrong, but it looks as though you'd entertain the idea of accepting the job."

She gave him her most scheming smile. "Ah, but Stephen, you're still operating on yesterday's program. In a very short time, you'll be on the seventh floor!" She waited for him to snap his fingers and say, "Gee, I hadn't thought of that."

But his reaction was quite different from what she'd hoped. "Anne, I don't think you really have a grasp of the situation. Regardless of what floor you're on, you'd still be employed by my firm."

"Yes, technically," she coaxed him. "But with you at one end and me at the other, that would no longer matter. We wouldn't be running into each other constantly, so it would make all the difference in the world. You see? Problem solved! Presto!"

"No," he said, "problem not solved. Quite to the contrary, problem just beginning."

"But Stephen, it really could be worked out if you'd only let it. This is what I've been hoping for. Praying for. This was the whole point in my coming to K&W to begin with—to get a job just like this one!"

He met her eyes with resolve. "And I don't see what stops you from doing just that, Anne. But clearly you can't be thinking of doing it at my firm." He shook his head as though the idea were preposterous.

"I'd sure consider it for a year, Stephen."

His expression was remote. "Look, I was barely able to justify all this sneaking around on a short-term basis with an end in sight. But now you're talking about a partner in a law firm blatantly smashing through rules he's taken a very strong part in making. I mean, think about that."

But Anne didn't want to think about that. She'd been hoping that some solution would rise out of nowhere, and the move seemed the perfect one. "Oh, come on, Stephen. You can't give me a choice between you and a position I can never get again!"

Her words seemed to hang in the air as she watched every muscle in his body slowly stiffen. "What does that mean?"

At all costs she hadn't wanted it to come out like this, but the time had come to tell him everything. Surely he'd understand once he knew how important it was to her.

"Stephen—" She sighed. "I'm afraid there are some things you don't know. I think we'd better have a talk." Anne walked over to the table and sat down.

"Look, maybe I didn't emphasize it enough," she began, "but law office management jobs really are almost impossible to come by. They rarely open up in the first place, and when they do they get filled before anyone even hears about them."

Anne put her hand on his arm in a silent plea for understanding. "Stephen, when Trudy told me that she was going to take a six-month leave of absence, she also told me that she . . . wasn't planning to return."

As he slowly set his glass down, Stephen's eyes bored intently into hers.

"We discussed it thoroughly," she continued, "and Trudy thought she could get me in as a temporary fill-in for her. On the rare chance that she did come back, well, that was one risk I was going to have to take. But if she didn't return, then I'd already be inside, and my chances of replacing her permanently would only depend on my performance. So I . . . I quit my own job."

Stephen stared at her in disbelief, and she lowered her eyes, suddenly wishing she'd told him all this in the beginning. "I was counting on the six months to prove myself, so that by the time they found out she wasn't returning, I'd have established a track record."

Stephen sat there stunned; he couldn't seem to comprehend her words. "Can you . . . get your old job back?"

"No," she whispered finally, raising her eyes to meet his. "Nor even one like it."

He shook his head in confusion. "Let me get this straight. You left a job you can't replace, to take a job you can't . . . replace?"

Anne nodded slowly. "Stephen, I know it sounds crazy, and I'm anything but a crap shooter, but slipping into a firm like K&W through the side door is a reprieve from heaven. A fluke. Another opportunity like this will never come up again as long as I live. And other than something like this, I have no way of competing with the people out there. It wasn't that way when I started six years ago, but things have changed. Today I'm just not that well qualified in comparison."

She squeezed his arm slightly as though to urge his compassion. "Obviously I hadn't counted on you coming into the picture. But now that you are, it just doesn't seem fair for you to give me a choice between you and my career."

Whatever she'd said, it seemed to toll a deep bell for Stephen. His eyes were on her, but he was seeing something else, and a long moment went by before he spoke again.

"You know something?" he finally said. "Based on the looks of things, you're absolutely right. I can't." His tone was one of hard irony.

Anne didn't like the look on his face. "What do you mean?"

"Well, you've just told me that under the circumstances, I have no choice but to back out of this whole situation right now, that's all." Stephen slapped his hand on the table, and it had a terrible sound of finality.

"What?" She couldn't believe her ears. "Stephen, why?"

"Because," he said, his temper beginning to surface as he got to his feet, "number one, I would never have started seeing you in the first place had I known you had any intention whatsoever of staying permanently.

"Second, I'm not going to be responsible for giving you any sort of ultimatum. As a matter of fact, you've just effectively prevented me from advancing anything that would even constitute an alternative, as long as it means you have to give up my firm's offer—namely, you tell me, your career."

She watched as the muscle in his jaw twitched. "And third, Anne, I can't believe you lied to me." He looked at his hand as if hoping to see an answer on it.

"*Lied* to you? What do you mean, I 'lied' to you?"

"Exactly that!" Stephen's anger finally unleashed, and the warm brown eyes that had always shown such tenderness were suddenly black and alienating. "All those times I mentioned the limited period you'd be at my firm, you never said one damned word about the fact that you weren't planning to leave at all. That's a rather clear-cut case of lying, wouldn't you say?"

She tried to interrupt, but he was hitting too close to home.

"Here all this time I was talking in terms of 'when,' and you weren't talking at all. Why? Because it wasn't 'when,' it was 'if'! Well, lady, that says our whole relationship is based on a lie!"

"What do you mean?" she gasped. "Even if I'd been able to put aside my own fears, I couldn't tell you! For one thing, Trudy hadn't officially made up her mind yet!"

Anne's own anger gathered momentum, and she hit out in the only direction she had left. "You forget, Stephen, you're a rather important part of the firm. A partner, no less! What am I supposed to do—take it upon myself to announce to someone at the firm that Trudy's thinking of not coming back? What if they lined up someone else, and then she changed her mind? Do I have the right to interfere with that?"

A dry smile of amusement surfaced before his rage dominated. "'Someone at the firm,'" he repeated under his breath. Then he exploded. "Fourth! You show absolutely no trust in me—what did you think I'd do, *call a partners' meeting*?"

"Stephen! Stop it! We don't even know for sure that they'll offer it to me! Why are we getting all whipped up at this point?"

But his eyes were like steel, and his words were delivered like delicate flowers of death. "Because at this point, my dear, unless they decide not to offer it on their own, your all-or-nothing crap shoot has blocked all my moves. Checkmate." He started to walk toward the door.

Anne ran to stand in front of him. "Stephen, what *difference* does any of it make? Why can't we just keep up . . . just like we are?"

Stephen looked at her, his voice clear and even. And lethally final. "Anne, your entire existence in my life is based on a false premise that you let me count on."

She crossed her arms defensively on that one. "I think I had some rather understandable reasons, if you stop and think about it."

The look in his eyes was one of helpless resignation. "Look, all that notwithstanding, this whole turn of events puts me in an impossible situation. From a professional standpoint I'm just not able to carry on a relationship with someone who works at my firm, skulking around like a thief in the night. It was uncomfortable enough while you were temporary, but—" Stephen shook his head, and suddenly Anne saw the very conservative partner of a very conservative law firm.

"Stephen," she pleaded, "if you cared about me you'd work it out. At least for a while. A year. That's all I need!"

Stephen looked at her sadly. "Oh, I care about you, all right. There's the irony."

Anne felt her face turn to stone. "So what you're saying is that I quit, or we break up. Is that it?"

He laughed as though she'd missed the whole point. "It's too late for that. Dammit, woman, *don't you see?*" He slammed his fist into his other hand.

"No, I don't *see.*"

"Look, I damned well won't be put in a position to give you an ultimatum—and then someday have it lurking behind every corner that you could have done this or that. I went down that road with Cathy—and never again! Not for you, not for me, not for anyone!

"Teaching ballet," he muttered. "That's a sick joke!" He suddenly looked as if he'd just tasted something bitter and then, holding up his hands, he pushed past her through the living room.

"Where are you going?"

"On down the road," he said. "I sure can't go down this one again."

Anne felt her blood turn to ice. "Well, if that's the only solution you can come up with, I can just as easily use your move onto the seventh floor to play out of sight, out of mind!"

His shoulders slumped at her words. "I just have no choices, Anne."

And opening the door, he left.

13

ANNE KNEW SHE'D NEVER forget the sound of that door. She listened to steady footsteps as they disappeared out of her life. She was stunned. Unable to comprehend what had happened. Too much had happened.

She sat down on the floor in the exact spot where she'd been standing, and she didn't move from it for a long, long time. Finally she became vaguely aware that darkness was falling. But it didn't matter.

All that mattered was that this wasn't some trite little misunderstanding. And it wasn't going to be patched up by retracting thoughtless words and phrases. This was real.

Thoughts roamed through Anne's mind in an endless array of distortions, playing cruel games with her every attempt to connect them. She had the vaguest feeling that she'd missed something important, but she'd been too wrapped in her own excitement to hear anything. All she could remember was that horrible resolve in Stephen's eyes.

Anne's mind wandered again. Tomlin. The firm. The move and the telephones. Designers and construction men. Evenings at Stephen's house. Onassis stretched out on his back. Stephen's ex-wife and how he had looked so closed when Anne had asked about her. What did Cathy have to do with Anne, anyway?

Pictures of little girls in tutus and ballet slippers suddenly danced through Anne's mind. Little girls with hopeful little eyes clumsily executing stiff pliés. The father Anne had never had. And the day her mother had started crying when Anne had asked for the thousandth time if she could take piano lessons. That day would never leave her memory. It was behind everything she'd become.

Her mother had just gotten home from work, and she was tired. So tired. Anne knew it was a bad time, but she wanted to ask just once more. Maybe her mom had been in a bad mood when she'd said no. She was always so exhausted, and sometimes just asking one more time would get a changed mind.

"Mom, isn't there any way I can have the piano lessons?" she had pleaded so hopefully. Oh, how she regretted that question now.

She recalled her mother standing there as she did the breakfast dishes Anne had left because she'd wanted to go play baseball. And how she stopped washing them so suddenly. Anne remembered looking at her back as she pulled her hands out of the dishwater and took the towel. She dried her hands and then slowly pressed the towel to her face. Anne would never forget the way her shoulders began to shake.

Anne was scared at first. "Mom?" she said. And then her mother turned around, and she was crying so hard that it made no noise. "Annie. Annie, I'd give *anything* to give you piano lessons. But don't you understand, honey? I *can't*. There's no money, I can't bring in any more, I can't turn to anyone for help, and . . . I can't even give my little girl piano lessons!" She buried her face once again in that dish towel. Anne remembered the sight of her shoulders . . . the way they just shook.

She rushed to her—by then crying herself. "It's okay, Mom. Please, Mom—it's okay. I didn't understand. Please stop crying, Mom, *please*?" Anne didn't know what else to do, so she just hugged her, tasting salt as she smacked little kisses against her mother's tears, trying desperately to make them stop coming.

Her mother laughed suddenly. Laughed through streaming eyes as she fought to gain control. It was the only time Anne remembered seeing her cry. Other than when her dad had died, of course.

As her mother pulled herself together she began to shrug off her reaction. She told Anne that she'd had a bad day and she was just tired, apologizing for having broken down like that, as if it were nothing to warrant a second thought. But Anne remembered the sight of her smiling through tears that still hadn't quite stopped coming.

They finished the dishes together, and Anne helped with dinner. They had Popsicles afterward, and her mother even pulled out Anne's baby pool so they could sit in the cool water to try to escape the heat.

By the end of the evening everything was back to normal. Her mother was in control again as if nothing had even happened. But Anne knew better. Nine-year-old Annie finally understood what it meant to be helpless.

Anne felt pinpricks in her legs now, and realized they'd fallen asleep while she'd been sitting on the floor. She slowly moved them to get the blood circulating again. Then her mind returned to Stephen.

Why couldn't he just give her time? A year was all she needed. Just a year. By then she'd be established as a law office administrator who had "arrived." And she'd have contacts. She'd have a solid career that could be taken anywhere. She'd never have to worry, no matter what unpredictable thing happened.

All the hours they'd already spent alone together . . . each had been perfect. "So perfect," she whispered to herself as a single tear fell down her cheek. So what would be wrong with another year of that?

Anne knew she didn't have the same feelings about "skulking around" that Stephen did. The one time they had gotten into a discussion about it, he had said that if a partner breached a policy like that, it would be considered a sign of "weakness and indiscretion that could have serious, far-reaching effects in the way he was viewed in general." Anne knew enough about the K&W brand of attorneys to know that was probably an understatement. Lawyers of that caliber and conservatism could be merciless over the slightest dent in anything bordering on ethics, and they had memories like elephants. Still, it wasn't as if she and Stephen were taking any risk. As long as they stayed at Stephen's house and her car was parked in his garage, what was the likelihood of being seen?

Suddenly a dry anger began to mount in her, and Anne slowly got to her feet. "Fine, Stephen," she said into the darkness. "To hell with you and your cat and your unwillingness to bend an inch. To hell with your 'image' in the partnership."

She reached over and flipped on the lamp in the living room, squinting as she waited for her eyes to get used to the brightness. Then she spun on her heel and went into the kitchen, slapping the wall switch on her way.

"So you aren't giving me an ultimatum, eh?" Anne scraped up the broccoli still spread out on the cutting board and tossed it into a bowl, piece by piece.

"And I've fixed it so you can't even offer me an alternative, eh?" She looked at the same stems and buds she'd so carefully chopped while Stephen was sitting at the table, but now the double portion seemed to mock her.

"Well, here's what I think about your position, Stephen!" Grabbing the bowl with her right hand, she threw it as hard as she could against the wall. She listened to the crash with perverse satisfaction as pieces of broken pottery became minced with green flowerettes on the floor.

Five minutes later Anne was in her car, taking the canyon curves with concentrated expertise. Instead of slowing down for Stephen's street, she accelerated, and continuing all the way to Wilshire, she turned west.

As the little car passed the office, Anne rolled up the windows and blasted the radio until she reached the familiar corner where she and Stephen always made a right-hand turn.

Anne got into the opposite lane. It wasn't a second after the light turned green when she squealed into a left turn, symbolically heading south. "Goodbye, Stephen!" she said. "I need more than a fair weather sailor."

Almost as though to challenge her statement, the deejay announced a song she'd listened to all too often on Stephen's patio. Anne immediately punched the button. Then, hearing another familiar tune, she punched it again. She'd punch that button all night long, even if she had to ram it through the dashboard.

PACIFIC COAST HIGHWAY changed names as it progressed through one beach city after another, until two hours later Anne found herself in Laguna. She'd finally gone far enough. Her mood had settled somewhat, yet by no means had it calmed. Quite to the contrary, it had cemented into stone.

Before turning around for the long drive home, Anne stopped at a café for some coffee. She watched a group of teenagers as they clowned around, flinging pieces of lettuce at one another. They looked so carefree.

Had she ever done that? No. She'd been too busy working her way through school so she could make something of herself. Was she supposed to throw out a gold mine of opportunity now?

Slamming down her coffee cup, Anne got into her car and headed back to Los Angeles. It was already late, so she took the freeway route. After all, there was some broccoli to clean up, and she wanted all signs of it, and everything it represented, out of the apartment—tonight.

THE NEXT MORNING Anne's first waking thought was that everything was still as it had been. But then her eyes snapped open. It wasn't.

She immediately got out of bed, knowing there was no way she could lie there thinking as she usually did. She couldn't work through aerobics or sit with the newspaper, either.

In fact, it was only a feat of sheer patience that got her through the agonizing forty minutes it took before she was out the door, listening to the click of her heels on the way to her car. They seemed to say, "That's that! That's that!" And somewhere in the far reaches of her mind, she replayed the sound to herself, all the way to the office.

Anne dived into her work with the door closed until eight-thirty, when the painters were supposed to arrive. Glancing at her watch, she went down to the seventh floor to see that they'd shown up with the right color. Sure enough, it was two shades too dark. "So lighten it," she simply said.

Three hours later the construction crew started to mark a wall in the wrong place. The more she argued, the more they humored her protests as though she were the cutest little child but very much in the way. Not in the mood for the hint of patronizing in their winks, she called the space planner.

He was there in no time. There had been a mistake on the plans, he finally admitted.

"Fix it!" Anne replied, handing him her pencil. Before he could close his mouth, she left.

The rest of the week was marked by a flurry of workers, installers, painters and carpet people, all tripping over one another in their attempts to stay out of each other's way. And particularly Anne's. She was determined to jam that completion date forward as fast as humanly possible, and she spared not a moment for bumbling. Instead she meddled and reorganized efforts at every turn.

BY THE LAST HOUR at the end of the week, the side of the suite that had been the executive offices was ready to move in to, phones and all, and the major partition wall separating the other side of the suite had been raised.

Meanwhile Tomlin had been working night and day on his appeal. He'd come across so many complex snags that he hadn't had time to stop in to see the progress, somehow contenting himself with Anne's daily assurances that things were going along just fine. Besides, he assumed, there would be little to see yet.

But late Friday afternoon, as everyone was leaving for the day, Anne stopped by his office to see if he was there.

"Come in, my dear," he said, creaking wearily back in his chair as she crossed the floor. "My! You look as tired as I feel. Is everything coming along all right?"

"Oh. I'm just fine," said Anne, taking her usual chair. She noticed he was looking at her as though he suspected something, and she didn't trust herself to leave any silences. She was beginning to feel too close to him.

"The executive offices are ready to move in to," she began, "and the loud part of the construction is done on the wall that separates K&W from the rentals. What would you think about the whole litigation department going to work on the seventh floor Monday morning?"

"Oh, pshaw," he said. Throwing his pencil on his draft, he rubbed his eyes. He didn't believe her.

Anne raised an eyebrow in mock challenge. "Come on. Take a break." She stood up.

Frowning slightly, Tomlin pulled his tired body to a stand and followed along to the elevator. Peering suspiciously at her expression as they dropped one floor, he mumbled, "You wouldn't try to make whoopie with a defenseless old man down in that empty shell, would you?"

Laughing, Anne led him through the enlarged reception room into the area where the executive offices had been. "Voilà," she said, holding out a hand.

"Good heavens!" he exclaimed, taking off his glasses as he walked down the hall and looked into each office. "And the phones?"

"Everything's in. It's ready." Anne looked down at the carpet cuttings on the floor. "Well, as soon as they vacuum, it will be."

"This is not possible. How did you . . ." He looked at her blankly.

Anne gave him an imitation of his own deadly look, squinted eyes and all. "I rode herd on them, Mr. Tomlin. I just got . . . crazed with power, and I drove them to their limits!"

"You can say that again," said a voice at the other end of the hall. The building manager was there, and he walked over to where they were standing, an expression of wary amusement on his face. He'd been out of town all week.

"So you're the young lady who has all these big strong men reduced to bowls of jelly." He looked at her admiringly.

Anne smiled ruefully. "I probably owe each of them an apology."

"Oh, I don't know. Instead of them playing one-upmanship with each other, I hear you had them all functioning like a space shuttle team preparing for a launch. In any event, it couldn't have been too bad, because they're all out having a beer together—paralyzed by shock and exhaustion but celebrating nevertheless." He laughed. "Are you sure I can't offer you a job?"

Anne sensed that Tomlin felt the awkwardness of the moment as much as she did. "Oh, well, at least you didn't ask if

I type." She said it in a kidding voice that got them all off the hook.

"So we really could move in this weekend," Tomlin said to himself, changing the subject. He began stroking his chin as though that were a whole new idea.

Anne blew a strand of hair out of her eyes. "I've already lined up one of the moving companies, just in case. I can cancel them, if you want—I have three more dates reserved with other companies." She looked at her watch.

He snapped out of his wonder, his eyes darting to hers. "No! By all means don't. Oh, but wait—obviously someone would have to be here to—"

"I will."

Tomlin looked at her with a curious little smile. Then, as though debating on whether to pursue the question in his mind, he hesitated a moment. "Doesn't a pretty young woman like you have something more interesting planned for a weekend?"

"Not this one, I don't." Anne pushed the strand of hair out of her face again, but she knew there was a slight plea in her eyes. She didn't try to hide it. Just as long as he didn't ask her to explain it.

Tomlin squinted, and his pupils seemed to drill right into her brain. "Hmm. Interesting. . . ."

He was getting too curious, and Anne dropped her eyes, not trusting herself to meet his any longer.

"Well," he said, testing, "if you think you can handle it by yourself, go ahead." That was a big statement. Anyone who knew attorneys would choose to bring lettuce leaves to a den of hungry lions rather than be responsible for a bunch of litigators arriving with their offices in boxes.

"I'm in the mood—why not?" she said flippantly.

Again that strange little smile stole from Tomlin, and he looked at the building manager, who was walking up and down the hall, peering incredulously into each office.

"Okay," he said finally. "If you feel up to it, it's all yours." He was still looking for a reaction.

"See you Monday," she said simply.

Sam and the other Xerox boy were still on the eighth floor finishing a late rush, and they happily agreed to work some weekend overtime. Anne asked them to be there at seven o'clock sharp. She'd have the coffee made and waiting.

AT SIX-FIFTEEN the following morning, Anne was sitting on the floor of the first office, drawing a sketch of the room exactly as it sat. She made it a personal challenge to see that each office would be packed and unpacked precisely as it had been found, down to the wall hangings and even the stacks of current work papers on the desks and credenzas.

There were eleven litigators in all, and she spent Saturday walking the movers through the duplication of each arrangement, handling the piles of paperwork and files herself. After testing her system, Anne showed the sketches to Sam and asked him to do the last two—Merrifield's and Butler's.

Sunday Anne passed the day in the library and the supply room, unpacking boxes and organizing every detail. Whenever her mind began to wander, she snapped it back to pencils and paper clips and to books and more books.

Finally, by nightfall, she took a hot bath and collapsed into bed with every muscle in her body aching. *Mission accomplished*, she thought. *Not a spare moment to think about Stephen. And soon he'll be right where I want him—out of my sight.* "Yes, out of sight, out of mind," she said, snapping off the light.

MONDAY MORNING WAS "HYSTERICAL," as Tracy put it. Anne stayed in her office, but as each litigator got out of the elevator, Tracy took great delight in stating, "You don't work here anymore." When they looked at her as if she'd lost her mind, she told them they'd been moved down to the seventh floor. In a state of shock, each got on the elevator and went down a flight, afraid of what would be waiting.

The general reaction was one of awe and amazement, with only one complaint. Lessinger just couldn't understand why he hadn't been called at home before his desk was placed.

The balance of the week was a relief. Not only had the computer suddenly gone down, which required extra time from Anne, but it really was as though Stephen had disappeared. Every time he seeped into her mind Anne pushed him back out with grave determination. She worked late every night and returned early each morning, operating on nervous energy that kept her flying. Until that Thursday, right after lunch.

ANNE WAS SITTING in her office, concentrating on a billing report that Tomlin wanted for the partners' meeting the following Monday night, when she overheard two of the associates talking as they walked down the hall.

"Oh, she's a knockout, all right. I met her once, and the girl's absolutely beautiful!"

"She's a school teacher, isn't she?"

"Mmm. Fifth grade."

"Well, it's been an interesting thing to watch. He's always been so quiet about his love life, I'll be curious to see if his savoir faire extends to women as well as courtrooms."

"You know, Cooper's tried to fix him up with that niece of his for ages now, and he's always begged off. I was floored at lunch to see the old man try once again. I expected Merrifield to utter one of his 'let's change the subject' routines, and what did he say? 'Okay.' That was it. Just 'okay.'"

Anne dropped her pencil in spite of herself. She stared straight ahead and listened to their voices trail off as they continued down the hall. She heard something about a Sunday barbecue at Mr. Cooper's house, but she went numb before she could hear the rest.

Slowly forcing her attention back to the billing report, Anne noticed that somehow it had become a bunch of unrelated numbers on a page. Fighting for control over her thoughts, she continued, anyway, making mistake after mistake, until the report was finally a smear of erasure marks. When five o'clock came, she quickly got her things together and left for the day.

Anne took the long route, suddenly dreading the solitude of her apartment. She'd done so well up to now. Was one overheard conversation going to devastate her?

Climbing the stairs like an automaton, she flopped down on the living room chair. So it was true. Stephen was going "on down the road," as he'd said. He really was walking out of her life as quickly as he'd entered it. Poof! It seemed impossible to believe, but there it was.

"Well, I can't keep up this mental three-ring circus forever," she finally admitted, speaking softly to herself. "I'll just have to deal with it. For all I know, he'd have done it later, anyway. Probably would have—nothing that perfect could have lasted."

Raising herself from the overstuffed chair, Anne kicked off her shoes on the way to the bathroom. The weather had cooled down a little, and a hot bath might help blank out her mind. Sometimes baths even changed moods, she thought grimly, pulling the faucet with a halfhearted yank.

Finally submerged in the warmth of her liquid cocoon, Anne decided she'd ride it out. Everything would eventually wear down and be less painful. The hurt of rejection always dissipated with time. All she had to do was wait.

"*So just let him go,*" she insisted out loud. But echoes don't lie, and there was no mistaking the crack she heard in her own voice. Suddenly hot tears began to stream down her face.

Angry with herself, Anne wiped them off with a wet washcloth as soon as they surfaced. But they just kept coming.

Finally giving up, she threw the washcloth and watched it stick to the wall for one brief second before it unpeeled, falling limply into the tub with an uneventful slosh. All pretense was now gone. It would be a night of mourning.

BY THE TIME ANNE WAS READY to face Friday, she'd regrouped her remaining strength, but the fervor that had seen her through the past two weeks had vanished. For the first time she arrived late to work.

With a calm resolve mustered, she finished her report and had Sam Xerox enough copies for each partner in addition to her own.

Leafing through them, Anne glanced over the names in the upper-right corner, and her eyes stopped cold on the word "Merrifield." Would she always do that? Or with the passage of time would she just glance on to the next.

In a moment of self-indulgence, she pulled out Stephen's copy and pressed it against her heart, as though it would give her a fleeting reprieve from reality. But then she caught herself. *Stop it! Just stop it!*

Quickly burying the report in the middle of the pile along with the others, Anne noted ironically that it lost its identity as soon as she couldn't see the name. Maybe there was some message to that, she mused bitterly, stuffing them into an inner-office envelope destined for Tomlin.

As the day neared its end, Anne began to think about the weekend. Maybe she should just get away for a couple of days. Sitting around the apartment would only remind her of the void, and she needed to rise above it, not to dwell in the murky emptiness.

Besides, now that Tomlin's appeal and the move were completed, minds would be turning toward resolving administrative matters. Trudy's job might even be one of the subjects at the partners' meeting. And either way that decision went, Anne would have to be prepared. Yes, the time had definitely come when she could no longer afford to think backward.

Just then, her phone rang. It was Tomlin.

"Hello, my dear. I was wondering. Can you arrange to stay late Monday evening?"

"Sure," she said lightly. "I have no plans at this point whatsoever."

"Er, the way this report is broken down, it might require some explanation, and since you've pulled together all the figures, I'd like to have you available so I could pop in and ask you questions if need be."

Anne swallowed. "I'm sorry if it's confusing. There's just been a lot happening over the past couple of weeks, and—"

"No, don't apologize. I know accounting isn't your strong suit. Just as long as one of us understands it," he teased. "Now you have a good weekend, eh?"

"Oh, I damned well plan to," she said, immediately surprised by the vehemence in her own voice.

"My!" laughed Tomlin. "That sounded rather—shall we say—seriously determined!"

And seriously determined it was, because with every mile Anne drove up the coast, she cemented her vow that by the time she returned, she was going to have Stephen and all thoughts of Stephen purged from her mind for good. Being a helpless, lovesick puppy had never been her style. All she had to do was remove him from her mental landscape. No more, no less than that. Simple. Lord, it felt good to begin seeing things so reasonably for a change! She took a deep breath of satisfaction as her thoughts turned to what she'd have for dinner.

What the hell, pondered Anne, passing the halfway mark to her destination. If Stephen's stupid standards were so damned important that he couldn't even break his own stupid rule for one short year, then how could he expect Anne to give up the one dumb chance she'd ever get, the most important standard she'd ever set for herself? She glanced at her watch. She'd been on the road for an hour and a half. If traffic continued as it was, she'd be in Santa Barbara in another hour and a half. Maybe she'd treat herself to a big order of crab's legs. That was it, crab's legs!

"Of course not!" snapped Anne, startling herself as the little Nissan pulled into the parking lot of the Santa Barbara Inn. "By Monday morning I won't care what kind of a time he had at Cooper's barbecue. I barely even care already!"

Slipping her car into the space, Anne looked at the image in the rearview mirror. "Then if that offer does come through by some hook or crook, Anne Michaels, there'll be nothing standing in your way. Nothing! Let alone a stupid ghost every time you see its blasted name on some stupid billing report! Right?" She grabbed her keys out of the ignition. "Right!" she said, climbing out of the car.

Anne meant to close the door firmly, but somehow it slammed, as if by a power of its own. *That's interesting*, she thought, sniffing the air. "Oh, well, back to dinner," she mumbled, heading across the parking lot. "Yes, let's see about that lamb chop I decided on!"

ON MONDAY MORNING Anne stopped to look at the flowers on the reception table at the office. Lingering for a moment, she touched a waxy petal as the elevator doors closed almost silently behind her.

Her face still felt a little raw from sunburn. She would never be fooled by an overcast day again, she swore. Especially if she was going to walk miles and miles on the beach.

Across the massive room, Tracy was on the phone whispering and laughing, still not yet aware anyone was present. Anne smiled to herself. It was an unspoken agreement they had. As long as Tracy kept being the best receptionist in the city, she could break up her empty hours with a personal call or two.

Anne pretended not to notice, returning her attention to the flowers. Particularly beautiful, this arrangement. She picked a small, browned tip off one of the leaves, and then she heard the abrupt click of the phone hanging up.

"Good morning!" Tracy called out, sounding as cheerful as ever. "Did you have a good weekend?"

"Yes. Actually, I guess I did," said Anne, aware that her voice sounded unusually serene. As she moved toward the inner door, she caught the look of interest on Tracy's expression, but she ignored it. Such a solid sound, oak flooring.

She ambled through the suite shortly after her arrival. The old litigation side was empty. Not a soul about. She headed toward it, strolling. One of the things that was supposed to be decided at the partners' meeting that night was whether to rent all the space out to sole practitioners with corporate-tax practices, as planned, or to hire a few extra paralegals until more associates could be recruited for K&W.

The ball was certainly rolling, Anne mused. The addition of a little unexpected space had started the partners thinking about expansion. It would be a megafirm in no time, she predicted. And all the better for its administrator.

Anne passed the place where Eileen's desk had been, and a little smile played at the corners of her mouth. She could almost hear the sweet, motherly voice echoing softly in the hall. "That Stephen. Nothing's been the same since he joined the firm."

The door to Stephen's old office was closed, and Anne opened it. Hesitating a moment, she went inside. Her eyes fell to the dents in the carpet where his desk had been, and she thought she noticed a faint trace of his scent that had lingered. Impossible, she decided. It was just her own memory playing tricks.

Tears threatened to well up in her eyes, and she immediately went out, closing the door quietly. *Remember, Anne, that's part of your deal with yourself. You don't get to look back.*

Heading toward her side of the suite, she continued to walk at an unhurried pace. As she passed one of the associates' offices, she heard the same voice she'd heard last Thursday. She could tell what he was talking about, and she didn't really want to hear. Still, she slowed down.

"Oh, she's in love, all right." The man whooped. "Did you see the way she looked at him when he arrived? I almost choked on a celery stick!"

Anne stopped walking and closed her eyes for a moment. Then a half smile of resignation slowly formed, and she went on her way.

Returning to her office, she spent the rest of the day working on loose ends from the move. That move, she reminisced. It had overshadowed all thoughts about all things.

Anne interrupted herself in midafternoon to check the supplies in the conference room. She didn't want to risk running into Stephen by doing it later on in the day. But just as she was arranging things on the massive conference table, the recessed spotlight over the doorway suddenly popped, leaving the entry barely illuminated.

A glance at her watch told her she probably hadn't caught it in time for the maintenance crew to be available, but she called the building manager, anyway. They were temporarily out of replacements, he explained, and it would be several days before it could be fixed.

"Oh, well," Anne said, wondering how a building could run out of spots, "I suppose we can survive without it. If anyone decides to trip in the doorway, what can they do—sue themselves?" She hoped he got the point.

When the partners began filing down the hall on their way to the meeting, Anne quietly closed her door. It was only after she was sure they were all tucked into the conference room that she felt safe to open her door again.

It would take them a while to chat before they got anywhere near the billing report, so she slipped into the ladies' room, taking a few extra minutes to dab some lotion around her eyes. They still looked a little red.

Finally Anne went back to her office and waited. Tomlin had promised he'd call her either way, so that if there weren't going to be any questions, after all, she could go home. Suddenly she felt very tired.

But only a few minutes passed before her phone rang. That was nice of him; he'd put the report first on the agenda. "This is Anne," she answered.

"Hello, my dear, could you please step in for a moment?"

Anne's heart jumped to her throat. *Damn!* Stephen was in there. Tomlin didn't know what he was asking. "Mr. Tomlin . . . is there any way I could explain it over the phone? I'm just—"

"No, my dear," he interrupted. "Please come in." He hung up.

Anne took a deep breath and gathered her courage as she headed for the conference room. She'd just avoid looking at Stephen, that was all.

"Sit down," said Tomlin kindly, offering the chair next to him.

Anne took the seat as her eyes scanned the faces at the table. A better look revealed that Stephen wasn't even in the room. She breathed a sigh of relief.

Tomlin began by asking whether the report included the current month, or if the break-off point had been the end of the quarter, just fifteen days prior. He was confused.

"No," she said, pointing at the dual totals. "I prorated the half month in parentheses to set it apart. Here's the grand total for all the time through last week." Why was she so sleepy? It was as if her mind was working in slow motion.

"Oh, I see," said Tomlin, laughing affectionately. "Usually parentheses mean some sort of deduction. I couldn't quite figure out what we were subtracting."

Just then the door opened. Anne's pulse quickened as a brief glance over Tomlin's shoulder confirmed that her worst fear had been realized. It was Stephen.

She could barely see him because of the darkened entry, but with her occupying the only extra chair, he leaned comfortably against the wall and waited. Within a moment his presence was forgotten by all except her.

Anne forced herself to think about the question Tomlin was asking, but as she explained the answer, her brain still seemed to be only half working. All she wanted in the world was to get out of there. Hopefully Stephen would have the grace to leave the doorway before she got to it.

After Tomlin had satisfied himself that he understood the format, he sat back and looked tentatively at one of the other partners and then back at her.

"Well, Anne, there's another matter I'd like to discuss with you while we're all together. It has to do with Trudy's decision." He cleared his throat.

Anne's heart skipped a beat as she glanced quickly around the table. Surely he wouldn't discuss anything personal other than in the privacy of his own office. But the other partners were expressionless, and she lowered her eyes to the report in front of her. It must be something related to it, she decided.

"I've received a number of calls from headhunters," Tomlin began, "and apparently there are some individuals with pretty significant qualifications who've expressed interest in coming with us."

Suddenly Anne was doubly thankful she'd run over every contingency in her mind. "I understand," she said simply.

"In any event— Well, frankly my dear, we've decided, after much discussion, to see if you'd be interested in the position."

Anne closed her eyes. But there it was nevertheless. The plum, right there in her hand.

"Trudy's salary was $40,000 a year when she left," he went on, "and though you're quite a bit less experienced on a few matters, you've certainly shown as much potential—and in some cases, equal or better work quality. So we've decided to start your salary at $35,000 as of tomorrow."

Anne swallowed hard. She'd made a lateral move to K&W for $28,000.

Tomlin seemed to find her silence understandable, and he continued, his voice soft and fatherly. "We'll give you some

time to acquaint yourself with the accounting functions, a
well as other areas you're light on. Then, once you're rea
sonably well versed in them, we'll go ahead and raise you t
the $40,000. Naturally you'll get the same perks Trudy had.

Anne stole a glance at Stephen. He was still leaning agains
the door with his arms crossed in a stance of deep concentra
tion. His eyes were glued to the floor as he listened.

She looked back at Tomlin, realizing he'd been patientl
waiting for her to say something, but suddenly she fel
tongue-tied.

"Mr. Tomlin," she began, "I've developed quite an affec
tion for this firm, and I—" her voice cracked just a bit "—
particularly enjoy working with you, and—" She felt a catc
in her throat.

"And I with you, my dear," he prompted. He looke
slightly bemused by her unexpected awkwardness.

Anne called on every ounce of control she could muster
and she finally met his gaze as evenly as she could. "Mr
Tomlin, I appreciate your offer, but . . . I can't accept."

A hush slowly fell over the room. "You . . . what?" Tom
lin's eyebrows drew together, and he looked at her incredu
lously. "But—"

Anne lowered her eyes as her voice became a whisper. "
just can't accept," she repeated.

Her almost inaudible words had cut through the silence a
though they'd been spoken into a microphone, and the re
port she'd been staring at slowly became blurred. *Don't,* sh
cautioned herself. *Whatever you do, Anne, don't.* But the
she saw a teardrop splash on the first page and watche
helplessly as it melted the ink-penned "Michaels" in the up
per right-hand corner.

Damn, she thought. *Not here, in front of everyone. Not i
front of Stephen.* She prayed for a small earthquake so tha
she could slip unnoticed out the door.

"But . . . but why?" asked Tomlin.

Anne could say no more, so she just shook her head.

"My dear," he persisted, "I'm sure the past two weeks have been unusually grueling for you, considering the move and all. But do look ahead," he urged. "With the litigation department just beginning to settle in on the seventh floor, why, soon it'll be as if they don't even exist, for all practical purposes. We're even thinking of delegating its workflow to one of the seventh-floor secretaries, since now you'll have subleasing to deal with. I'm sure things will get a little easier if you just give it a little time."

Tomlin's statement was uncanny in its innocence, and Anne couldn't resist shooting a look of irony in Stephen's direction. "Considering all that's involved, I really feel this is the best decision for everyone concerned. Myself included."

Stephen suddenly cleared his throat. "Harold, it looks like she's turning us down." He didn't move from his pensive position, but as he'd been so silent and separate from the group, his words seemed to cut through the room like a knife.

Annoyed Tomlin turned toward him. He wasn't used to getting short-circuited by anyone. "Stephen, you've made such a point of expressing no opinions on this matter," he berated him. "Must you pronounce premature conclusions now?"

"I'd just like to ask a question or two before we accept her answer, that's all." Surprisingly, Stephen's tone betrayed equal agitation, which deepened the hushed tension in the room. He ignored it. "Anne, I just wanted to be sure this is something you want, independent of any outside influences."

She closed her eyes. *Stephen, why are you doing this?* But she willed her voice to remain steady. "Yes, I'm sure. I just think it would be better if I just . . . go on down the road."

Tomlin's eyes bored into Anne's. "Is that what's bothering you? That some of the partners didn't think you were ready to handle the job on a permanent basis? Because if it is," he hastened to continue, "we're prepared to give you all the time you need." There was a general murmur of agreement around the table, which only served to spur him on. "So then, given that fact, I just can't for the life of me, understand any reason why—"

"Excuse me, Harold," Stephen persisted. "Back to outside influences, Anne." He was now taking it a little too far, and all Anne's pent-up emotion would soon find an outlet in anger.

She looked at him a long moment. "Look. I have just been given an official offer," she said evenly. "Under the circumstances I'm free to accept it or not, depending upon how I assess my own...'strengths,' if you will. Frankly, up until Friday I thought I'd be able to handle it quite well, as a matter of fact. But now, on further thought, I just don't feel I'm up to all that's required. And to put you at ease, it's my decision, and it's free of 'any outside influences,' as you put it. Now does that satisfy your question, or do you have more?"

Suddenly Stephen exhaled deeply, collapsing his shoulders as though he'd just won a hard-fought match. "Will you marry me?"

Anne's eyes squeezed involuntarily shut in stunned disbelief as Stephen's words fell on the room like a bomb. There was a moment of motionless silence, and then Tomlin's pencil dropped onto the table with a weak little splat.

"Anne?" urged Stephen, ignoring everyone else as if they didn't exist.

She opened her eyes and slowly looked at him. He was just standing there, waiting for her answer.

Time seemed to freeze as every eye in the room turned to her, then to Stephen, then back to her.

"You're...insane," she finally whispered. Anne wasn't fully aware that she'd spoken until after the words had come out; but even then they seemed to have come from someone else.

"Oh, dear... I thought there was something," said Tomlin, slowly beginning to recover. "So that's—" He stopped the sentence. "Oh, dear *me*," he repeated, laughing softly as he scratched his head. Then he quietly cleared his throat. "Gentlemen, let's take a short recess, shall we?" There was a delicacy in his voice that defied any words to be spoken, and he pushed his chair back with a gentle shove.

Sitting in shock, Anne covered her eyes with one hand, but she heard a number of long, deep sighs followed by a general shuffle of chairs and feet.

Finally she peered up through her fingers as the procession took its awkward leave. Stephen had already opened the door, and he simply stood aside as partner after partner filed past him into the corridor. The man seemed totally oblivious to what he'd just done. Either that or he didn't care, because each of their astonished glances met with nothing more apologetic than a look of tolerant patience as he waited for them to empty the room.

As soon as the last of them had left, Stephen closed the door ever so quietly. Then there was silence.

Anne stared at him blankly from where she sat, unable to believe what she'd just witnessed. Her hand had slowly lowered from her forehead until it was just hanging limply in midair.

"Stephen, would you mind explaining—" She shook her head, at a loss. This couldn't really have happened. Not really.

Stephen closed his eyes and took a deep breath. "Anne, there's something I've never been able to tell you about, and when I really needed to, the timing was impossible."

He crossed the room and took Tomlin's chair, turning it so that he could face her. There was a grave seriousness in his eyes.

"Anne, just before Cathy and I were married, she walked out on a career as a dancer to move to Los Angeles with me. She'd been given an offer to join one of the best ballet companies in New York, and...I talked her into turning it down." There came that familiar look of pain in his eyes, only this time he didn't try to hide it.

"Cathy had spent her whole life working toward something and, to me, dancing just seemed like a pastime of fun and play, so there was no question about whose work came first. I accepted an offer here. And that's where I was going, with or without her.

"Given those alternatives, she chose to come. But walking out on something she'd lived for all her life destroyed her."

Suddenly Anne recalled the words she hadn't understood in her kitchen: "I damned well won't be put in a position to give you an ultimatum." And that other time, the way he'd winced when he'd said, "If training someone else to be a prima ballerina is something you've always longed to do . . ."

"But Stephen, I'm not Cathy. Why would you feel you couldn't even suggest anything that would constitute an alternative?"

A sardonic little laugh escaped. "Once you'd told me how much you'd risked? Once I'd seen the qualifications on the résumés that have been flooding Tomlin's desk?" He shook his head. "Listen, Anne, I love you, sweetie, but I picked up a couple of those résumés and looked them over, and you were right. Your background is child's play compared to what I saw on them. I realized that with more guts than common sense, you'd knowingly gone out on a skinny little limb, and the bottom line was that I was sitting on the only apple you could reach."

"But Stephen," whispered Anne, "you didn't give me a chance. Why didn't you just tell me all this then? That night at my apartment—"

"God, Anne, don't you see the parallel? What was I going to say? 'Dear Anne, I can't carry on a relationship with someone at my firm because it would involve lying to my partners. On the other hand, you've just told me your career depends on staying at my firm. So take your choice. Me or your career.' Ah . . ." He sighed bitterly. "Cathy all over again."

"That's the 'checkmate'?" It had been an odd little reference when she'd first heard it, and she wondered why she hadn't questioned it. "But why didn't you just explain all this? Right then and there?"

Stephen laughed. "Anne, I initially left in anger because I felt I'd been lied to. But once I thought about it, I also saw that explaining it would, in itself, constitute giving you an ultimatum. You see?"

"So you backed out?"

"Yeah! Till you made your decision, you bet I backed out!"

She held up her hands. "But what's so different now? I still had to choose."

"Nope, wrong," he corrected, sitting back in his chair. "With me out of the picture and making no moves, you only had K&W. You were free to accept Tomlin's offer or not, as you saw fit. The difference is that I wasn't there to influence it."

"Oh, sure." She grimaced. "With your ghost lurking around every corner, I'm supposed to function."

Stephen crossed his arms. "Ah, but a ghost is something that can only live in your mind. Is it reality? Or is it an illusion? Only you could determine the importance of that."

Anne stared at him. "Have you been studying some Eastern philosophy or something?"

"Nope, just the same old chessboard. You see, there was one square left, retreat and wait." Stephen smiled smugly. "Your move."

Anne's mouth dropped open on that one. "Well, a terrific little game you've got there, Stephen! When I drove out of Los Angeles Friday night, my one and only thought was 'To hell with him.'" She waved a hand in angry, uncaring dismissal.

Stephen nodded as though he fully understood her feelings, but then he frowned slightly. "I just have to know. What was the turning point from such a reasonable conclusion?"

Anne glared. "Oh, there were several things. They bounced around in my head all weekend, as a matter of fact! Try Cooper's niece for starters. 'A knockout!' 'Oh, she's in love!'" Anne imitated the partner she'd overheard. "Can you imagine a year of having to hear the details of your love life?" She gritted her teeth. "Your associates really aren't very discreet, you know."

"I know," he said, an amused smile breaking through, and Anne stared at him in disbelief.

"What's so damned funny?"

The grin continued to widen into one of sheer delight. "Oh, I figured word would surely get around. I thought if jealousy could rear her little green head on my behalf . . . well, I didn't have much else going for me, now, did I?" Stephen looked as though he'd just swallowed the birdie . . . whole.

Anne turned her head slightly away, still holding his eyes. "Oh, come on, that couldn't have been . . . contrived."

Stephen shrugged, looking apologetic. "Well, I admit, it can't be called a terribly imaginative strategy. But it did seem fairly . . . reliable, shall we say? After all, Greg's been like a puppy at Cooper's door ever since he first saw the young lady, and the one fault we can't seem to break Greg of is that he always advertises his opponent's gains."

Anne looked at him a long moment, evaluating. "That's really farfetched, Stephen."

He laughed. "Look, what's a fellow to do when he only has a ghost on his side? Stephen held out his hands in a gesture of innocence. "You didn't have to respond, you know. You could have decided I wasn't that important to you, after all."

"I'm not quite sure you're not making all this up, Stephen."

"Look, could I make this up? I got desperate! Pure and simple!"

"Desperate, eh? Well, I did gather that 'the young lady,' as you put it, is quite beautiful. Certainly that must have made it just a tad easier for you."

"Extremely beautiful," he agreed. Stephen took a deep breath. "I really hoped you'd hear about that part." The mischievous twinkle came back into his eyes. "Naturally I made sure there were plenty of people around to see her."

He was just a little too exuberant and self-satisfied to be faking it. "Are you telling me that this whole two weeks, while I've been running around like a chicken with my head cut off, you've actually been quietly sitting back plotting my demise?"

He raised an eyebrow as the look of amusement faded somewhat. "Well, if my ghost hadn't worked, it might have been my demise, because I know I wouldn't have been able to tolerate yours lurking about."

Anne shook her head. She felt as if she'd been put through a sieve. "Stephen, why in the world hadn't you said anything about our future before this job offer came up? All those evenings at your house, when we talked about how we felt about each other . . . you never said anything."

His mouth dropped open. "God, woman! Do you have any idea about the look on your face whenever I said anything that had to do with Trudy's return? Every time I started to bring it up, wham! We were onto another subject."

Anne stared at him for a moment, and then her hand fell onto the table with a resigned thud. "Well, so much for avoidance," she said with a grimace.

But suddenly a burning curiosity was reflected in Stephen's eyes. "Incidentally—I just have to ask. After turning down Tomlin's offer, what had you decided to do?"

Anne looked down at the report in her lap, and she curled the corner into a little roll. "Wing it," she said. "Actually, I found out that there's a little group of managing partners who meet from time to time. Tomlin's in the group, and I thought maybe . . . who knows." She raised her eyes to his. "It didn't look overly promising," she admitted. "But I know he likes me, and he is pretty good at pulling strings."

Stephen put his head in his hands. "My, you do take crap shoots."

"Well, you're certainly no slouch, dammit. What if I'd accepted?"

He was just about to answer when the sound of voices came from far down the hallway.

"Oh, God," said Stephen, suddenly remembering. He covered his eyes with his hand.

"Stephen, forgive me for saying this," Anne said quietly, "but that was a rather amazing move on your part. I mean, you slam out of my apartment in a froth because you can't let your partners know you're dating someone in the firm. And then, at the eleventh hour, you step out of a darkened doorway and ask me to marry you in front of each and every one of those same damned partners! What in the world could you have been thinking?"

Separating two fingers, he peered at her with one eye. "Want to know the truth?"

She nodded.

Stephen closed his fingers again. "It's just that sometimes I get these . . . impulses! I really *can't* control them," he complained.

"Oh, God," Anne pleaded, rolling her eyes. "What am I getting myself into?"

"Merrifield!" came a shout. "We're going home, you crazy bastard."

Stephen winced. "Yeah—uh, thanks!" he called. "I appreciate that!" But then he glanced back at Anne, looking a little more ruffled than he'd sounded. "I suppose it wasn't what one could call my most well-thought-out moment," he admitted. He scratched his head. "As a matter of fact, this one may take some serious undoing."

As the sound of people in the hallway diminished, there was a soft knock at the door.

Stephen glanced at Anne with knowing dread in his eyes. "Come in," he sighed, getting to his feet.

Tomlin entered and walked toward them, shaking his head. Then he clasped Stephen's hand between his two. "Stephen, my boy, you really had me worried. You've been so silent lately that I thought a whole month was actually going to go by without some absolutely unacceptable disruption from you."

Stephen flushed. "How could I disappoint you, Harold?"

Tomlin stared at him. "Couldn't you try?" he begged. "*Just once?*" His tone was almost desperate.

But in the next moment he turned toward Anne, his eyes softening. "As for this young lady," he said, "I dare say she's become as close to my heart as you have, my boy."

Tomlin gave Anne's shoulder an affectionate squeeze. "She's certainly given me less trouble—" Then he considered a moment. "Oh, dear, I forgot about her sense of humor," he added. "Actually, this match could have some disastrous ramifications when I think about it."

But after a moment he grew serious. "Anne," he began tentatively, "you told me once that your father was... deceased?"

"Yes," she said.

He hesitated again, looking almost shy. "Well, I'd certainly be honored to give you away at your wedding."

In one sentence Tomlin had done it to her again, and afraid to trust her own voice, Anne just nodded.

He looked at her for a long moment and then abruptly cleared his throat. "Well! I'm afraid this has been a rather exciting day, children. I think I'll just 'go on down the road,' as you say."

But he only got as far as the door before he stopped cold. "No, I simply can't resist," he said. "Stephen, that was a rather telling phrase Anne chose. I went 'tilt' at that point, and it was only my obsessive nature that kept me from putting together immediate conclusions. But now that I think about it, I should have suspected sooner."

Stephen frowned and looked at Anne, but he only saw curiosity mirrored in her eyes. "Why?"

Tomlin slowly turned to peer at them over his glasses. "That day in my office. She wasn't a bit intimidated by Cooper. But she treated you just like a fragile egg." He raised an eyebrow, shaking his head as though it had all been just too transparent.

Stephen cleared his throat. "Do you think there's going to be any problem with this, Harold?" There was now valid concern in his voice.

Tomlin just sighed tiredly. "No, my boy, I've already taken care of that in a little hallway conference of my own just now."

Then his stance became unmistakably lawyerly. "You see, technically Anne Michaels never was actually employed here, was she. I mean, to you and I, Stephen, such a point would seem obvious to even the most casual observer. But if there's ever any question, well, the temporary payroll records illustrate that fact quite clearly, I'd say."

Tomlin paused just long enough to look at each of them as though they represented the source of a potential heart attack, and then he turned once again toward the corridor. "Good night, children."

They listened as his footsteps faded farther and farther away, until the reception door opened and closed again. Then there was silence.

Anne lifted her eyes to Stephen's, and in one look they exchanged what would have taken a lifetime of words to say. At last he simply held out his hand, and in the next moment Anne was once again surrounded by the warmth that had become but a dream.

It seemed forever since he'd held her that way, and she buried her face in his chest. She felt like laughing, she felt like crying. But she couldn't do either. She just hugged him to her, wanting never to let him go again.

"Let's get out of here," Stephen finally whispered.

Stopping in Anne's office only long enough to get her purse off the desk, they continued slowly down the hall toward the lobby.

Stephen loosened his tie as he draped an arm around her shoulders. "So your answer is yes? You never did tell me."

"Well, that depends." Anne pondered. "I assume you have no objections to a working wife."

"Oh, damn!" He clutched his forehead. "Does that mean I have to keep helping with the dishes?"

"Only for two or three years. Just till I get a reputation for unquestioned brilliance."

"Or till baby number one is born. That's what you said over our first glass of wine together, I recall."

"Well, let's see. What's the terminology again? 'Until
minimum of three years shall have passed, or until said chil
shall have been born, whichever first occurs?'"

"It would go something like that," he mused. "Okay, I hav
no objections, but let's get Tomlin busy finding you a nev
arena tomorrow. So now, back to your answer." He waited

Anne laughed slightly. "Yes, Stephen Merrifield. I wil
definitely marry you."

He smiled. "When?"

"Tomorrow."

Stephen snapped his fingers. "Oh, wait a minute. I have
hearing in division 2. It could take all day."

"Mmm. The next day, then."

"Okay, you're on."

Anne shook her head slowly, thinking over the past two
weeks. "Stephen, I really do love you. I really, really do."

"I know," he whispered.

Harlequin Temptation

COMING NEXT MONTH